F

The
Doctor's
Daughter

The
Doctor's
Daughter

Elizabeth Seifert

Thorndike Press • Chivers Press
Thorndike, Maine USA Bath, England

This Large Print edition is published by Thorndike Press, USA
and by Chivers Press, England.

Published in 1997 in the U.S. by arrangement with
Blassingame-Spectrum Corporation.

Published in 1998 in the U.K. by arrangement with
the author's estate.

U.S. Hardcover   0-7862-1250-0   (Candlelight Series Edition)
U.K. Hardcover   0-7540-3161-8   (Chivers Large Print)

The text of this Large Print edition is unabridged.
Other aspects of the book may vary from the original edition.

Set in 16 pt. Plantin by Juanita Macdonald.

Printed in the United States on permanent paper.

British Library Cataloguing in Publication Data available

Library of Congress Cataloging in Publication Data

Seifert, Elizabeth, 1897–
    The doctor's daughter / by Elizabeth Seifert.
       p.   cm.
    ISBN 0-7862-1250-0 (lg. print : hc : alk. paper)
    1. Large type books.   2. Physicians — Middle West
— Family relationships — Fiction.   I. Title.
[PS3537.E352D63   1997]
813'.52—dc21   97-39744

The
Doctor's
Daughter

Chapter 1

My name is Joey Fivecoat — well, not now, but to begin this record, I have to start with that. And I do want to put certain things on record. For myself, and for those who come after me. Alice Peck never will do it, and of course Tread can't. So . . .

My name is Joey Fivecoat. When I was born, the name given me was Joie, a sentimental name bestowed on their first baby by my delighted young father and even younger mother. I can picture them — the tall, blond young Dr. Fivecoat and his lovely chestnut-haired wife.

Perhaps they named me while Mother was still in the hospital, perhaps they waited until they had me at home, and made the decision bending over the helpless, sleeping infant in her net and ribbon decked bassinet. I was to see that same bassinet, refurbished, in use for Treadway, my brother, and, two years later, for Alice Peck.

At any rate, the name Joie was chosen for me. But no sooner had I entered kindergarten — the exclusive, small kindergarten conducted by two elderly sisters of impeccable social standing, but in what was then called "reduced circumstances" — than the other children changed it to Joey. And certainly this became my name when I did go to school. What American child, however well behaved, was going to call anyone Joie?

So my name is Joey, and I am glad. I am the eldest of the three Fivecoat children. I was a small, blonde child, with big, dark eyes, and thick eyelashes. Not so much pretty as noticeable. My mother was pretty. She still is. Beautiful.

My story has to do with the way we grew up, and what happened to us. With a way of living we thought wonderful, and in some respects, it was wonderful; in some respects, the result seems to be good.

It began in the forties, during and after World War II; Korea had not yet become a troublesome problem. There were no lettuce boycotts in those days, no movement to liberate women, and certainly no student rebellions.

Children, too, were different in those days. One set of rules served for everyone — rules that were firmly formulated by the time I was born and kicked my rosy little heels in that white net and pink ribboned bassinet in the nursery of the tall house on Lockwood Terrace.

My father had a plan for his life. Whether this was a continuation of the life which he had known with his parents, or was a plan that would correct certain difficulties in that life, I really do not know. I vaguely remember my grandfather, but my grandmother was dead by the time I was born. They were people of substantial means; they had lived in our home before we did.

And perhaps my father's plan was to continue the pattern set by his ancestors, marred by an occasional wrong-colored thread, perhaps, but essentially a life of beauty and grace.

We children were born, and grew up, as a part of that tapestry. We grew up to a standard of cold showers, huge, soft, white towels, and firm beds with white linen sheets and satiny comforters from Plummers. Our table linens were white, and monogramed.

Still remembering the depression and bound by the strictures of wartime, my father saw to it that we had everything we needed and that he wanted us to have. He had hated Roosevelt and was still fulminating against him when I reached an age to pay attention to such things. He disliked President Truman, he deplored the war in Korea and its every aspect; rationing seemed to be as horrible a crime as the killing of young men and the bombing of England.

I now believe that neither the depression nor the war had really touched my father. His own parents had protected him. During the war he was in medical resident training and exempt from service.

I judge his childhood by the one he gave to his children. It was a sheltered childhood, and a loving one. He made a picture of his home, and one of his family as well. We never quarreled, because a harsh word was not permitted, a resentful act was sorrowfully reproved. We loved one another, in appearance and in fact. Our behavior was too carefully regulated for there to be friction. The picture must always be perfectly maintained. There could be no criticism. The rooms of our home looked like rooms pictured in a fine magazine, our clothes and our behavior must maintain that ideal, and did maintain it. The picture was set, we lived in it, we were a part of it.

But was it really ideal? That home and that life? When it was destroyed, I could say that, yes, indeed it had been. My father never believed that he had destroyed the picture. Perhaps he had not, and I suppose this belief made for his continued personal contentment.

★ ★ ★

In any case, as children we lived in that picture home, a tall town house on Lockwood Terrace, a house built of pink brick with white stone trim, a terraced lawn and shrubbery on the street side, behind it a landscaped lawn and garden entirely enclosed within an ivy-grown wall, the gates kept locked. There were moss-grown brick walks in that garden, low, clipped boxwood hedges, roses and flowering bushes trained to arch above the walk. A fairyland place for children to inhabit. We children attended exclusive schools, our friendships and our lives were selectively maintained in a rarefied strata of air "above society."

We had our pleasures on the same level. We went on picnics with hampers packed and stowed in the trunk — or "boot" — of the current car, and the picnic feast spread in the woods or beside the stream owned by some friend of the family, never in the public park or where crowds of people might observe or intrude.

We had, and enjoyed, suppers informally served in our garden. We attended, and enjoyed, cookouts at Uncle Doc Winter's home out in the country, where we children became what my mother called rowdy with his nephews and niece, and our clothes became

11

rumpled and soiled. We generally spent Christmas with Uncle Doc, too, in his wonderful home, again with the only family he had. How I did love Uncle Doc and his big, comfortable home! I thought the blazing fire on the big hearth much better than the tidy little fires on the marble hearths of Lockwood Terrace. I liked books piled in the corner of a room, and a bushel basket of his own apples set out, in contrast to the fruit bowl on the polished mahogany dining table at our home. Two apples, two oranges, a banana, a cluster of green grapes, one of red. A child could get permission to take fruit from that bowl, and his selection was always immediately replaced. It was good fruit, carefully washed and peeled for us. But it never was quite as satisfying as one of Uncle Doc's apples.

Uncle Doc heaped chrysanthemums into a great brown jar, he hung branches of bittersweet from the knocker on his front door. In our home we had blue iris and daffodils in a gray ceramic vase, pink roses and baby's breath in a silver bowl. . . .

I remember once saying to my mother that I liked Uncle Doc's house and the things we did there. She smiled patiently at me and smoothed my pale hair. "People live in different ways, Joie," she told me. "Dr. Winter is a large and hearty man; we all love him dearly. But we also love your dear father, whose tastes are different."

Yes, we did love our father. I certainly did. His fresh-colored face, his blue eyes behind their shining spectacles, his blond hair, his meticulous clothes, his very clean hands . . .

I loved my mother, too. I loved her very dearly. Her name was Christine, and I used to wish I had been named for her. She was a lady in every way, and entirely submissive to her husband, whom she adored. I thought she was pretty, and I believe she was. She was a small woman, who moved neatly, who never raised her voice, but who could grieve deeply when hurt, and hardly recover from that hurt.

We were a close family; we did many, many things together. Carefully planned to the last detail, we took trips together. By car, sometimes, to Wisconsin or Minnesota in the summer. We stayed at large hotels. Once we rented a home on the seashore and took our cook with us. We stayed there for a month.

We went to England on an ocean liner; we went by rail to Canada and a beautiful lake there. I liked train travel very much, but it made Tread and Mother motion-sick.

We did happy things in our home. There

was a billiard table on the third floor and we played together up there. We played backgammon before the library fire, setting up a tournament. Our father always won these, as, he explained, was to be expected. He had played much longer than we had.

One winter we decided to try our hands at painting, putting on smocks, and being instructed about oil paints, charcoal and chalk. None of us turned out to be very good at this except Alice Peck, who enjoyed it the most, and, at that age, splashed paint over everything.

Another winter we all learned to skate, and enjoyed that when we could go to the lake in the park. We children never were allowed to go without our parents.

One family expedition, I particularly remember. This was carefully planned, too, but by Uncle Doc, not our father. He never was enthusiastic about that trip.

"Oh, Paul, for Pete's sake!" Uncle Doc would cry. "Let down your hair a little. . . ."

"Christine could not stand such a trip."

"I agree. So let her stay at home, enjoy a week of peace and quiet without you and the kids. But those same kids, Paul, can't grow up in this state and not know the mountains and the rivers fifty miles away from this city. They must take at least one float trip. If they

14

don't like it, they need never go again. If they do, I've started a fine thing for them."

"Sometimes," said our father, "I wonder why you and I are friends."

"I wonder the same thing, often," said Uncle Doc heartily.

He was a hearty man, a tall man, and somewhat heavy, though never fat. I first remember him as nearly bald, with a fringe of white hair. He wore horn-rimmed spectacles, his skin was as pink as a baby's, and we all loved him very much.

And we did make that trip by john boat and canoes with him, the four Fivecoats, with Alice Peck falling into the water at least once a day, and the Winter children, Philip, Alan and Cynthia, all about the same age as we three.

I loved the whole experience, the silky brown water, the white foam and black rocks of the rapids. Father kept insisting that we portage these, but Uncle Doc and the guides got us through. I loved the high sandstone cliffs, the overnight camps on the sandbars at the foot of them — fish and bacon and eggs cooked over a campfire, the noises of the night — Alice liked it, too, but Father and Tread did not. They talked only of mosquitoes, chiggers, and wet shoes.

I knew at once that the trip would not be

repeated, and I was sorry.

And I, too, began to wonder why Father and Uncle Doc were such good friends. Of course they were both doctors and shared medical offices. I am pretty sure that they had known each other in medical school, or perhaps when they were residents. Uncle Doc had been active in the war, serving in the Pacific, I believe. He was a little older than Father. A bachelor. His family consisted of his brother's children. Their mother had married a second time. I once asked if that marriage had ended in death or divorce, and my father had asked, softly, if it mattered. The Winter kids didn't live with Uncle Doc, but they nearly always were around when we were. I think this annoyed my father. I didn't know why; they were nice kids.

We went frequently to Uncle Doc's — oh, about six times a year. He lived out in the country. And Uncle Doc often was in our home. For one thing, we lived near the big Medical Center where he was a Staff orthopedic surgeon, and just across the wide boulevard from the Medical Arts Building — a handsome, three-story edifice, with all sorts of luxury shops on either side of it. My father and Uncle Doc had their offices on the third floor, with Uncle Doc's rehabilitation rooms, the lab and X-ray rooms using the rest of the space up there.

On many evenings, finished with their office duties, Uncle Doc would come home with Father, and the two men would have a drink in the library, or out in the garden if the weather were warm. Sometimes he would stay for dinner. I used to love to tuck into a deep chair in the library and listen to the two men talk. I was especially fascinated when that talk dealt with medical matters, and it very often did. There are certain things like the vagus nerve that, for me, will always be associated with the smell of fine leather, wood smoke, lemon peel and rum.

Uncle Doc was an orthopedic surgeon, a specialist. My father was an internist, an ulcer specialist. He dealt with every digestive situation which could and did lead to ulcers of the tract.

After an hour of listening to the men talk, I always had to spend another hour with the dictionary. I remember confusing the word "tract," Which they used so often, between the alimentary system and religious pamphlets. Both men would have laughed heartily had I revealed my confusion, but then I was embarrassed by my ignorance. I wanted to listen to them talk. I did listen, whenever I could escape from Tread and Alice, or from my mother's vigilant eye. I believe the men knew I was there. If they gave my presence any thought, it would be to decide, "She'll get bored and fall asleep."

I clearly recall the evening when they talked freely of a medical meeting which Father had attended in Chicago. A surgeon — "a gentle, stooped professor of surgery" at some medical school — was treating patients with severe, stubborn stomach and intestinal ulcers by cutting the two vagus nerves that served those areas.

"Success with ninety-five out of ninety-seven cases!" my father reported exultantly. "Think of that, Dick!"

"How long since . . . ?"

"Well, three years at the most, but . . ."

"The things have a cycle of five-year return, Paul."

This made my father impatient. "I know, I know! But I am inclined . . ."

"Be careful," said Uncle Doc.

"But there are cases, Dick, when being careful is not enough! Diet, even surgery — the blasted things come back!"

"Psychoanalysis, maybe?"

"Maybe. Though it doesn't work for a certain type of people. The ulcer type, for one. And don't suggest a change of occupation for the patient I have in mind."

"The senator."

"Yes, indeed. If this operation would drastically reduce his outflow of gastric juice . . ."

"Would you attempt it yourself or send the man to your gentle, stooped professor?"

"I could do it."

"Oh, sure you could, Paul. And it might work, too."

"I'd give the patient a choice."

"I think that would be right," said Uncle Doc.

I found such a discussion as fascinating as any mystery or adventure story. I wanted, desperately, to find out if Father did operate on the senator, and — I could have asked Uncle Doc. I realize that now. He would have respected the validity of my interest, and answered me. But I was then only twelve, and Father would have considered such an interest not precisely what a tenderly raised *jeune fille* should possess. He had some very strict ideas about *jeunes filles*.

And about other things. Uncle Doc laughed at him and his queasy dislike of off-color stories, of the growing permissiveness of child-rearing, of the arrogance of servants — that meant anyone who served him. Uncle Doc called him the last of the aristocrats, and hoped he would never hear him cry, "Off with their heads!"

But the civil rights law as first passed made my father concerned to the point of illness. He called it an invitation to a spreading infection. . . .

"You'd better learn to live with it, and keep quiet as well," advised Uncle Doc.

I think Father did learn to do both things. As I watched this painful learning, as I myself grew older, I admired his air of patience, and of thinly veiled exasperation with an over-friendly taxi driver, a careless waiter, or a rude doorman. Not speaking, Father could convey his opinion of such things.

Remembering those times, I see my father always in the spotlight of our family stage. He was the star. But at his side, or seated behind him, I always see my mother as well. She was a quiet woman, she was pretty — at times, she could be beautiful. And always, always she was proper. She wore the correct clothes, she said the proper things, and did the proper things.

Above all else, she adored my father. It was she who put him in the spotlight, and kept him there. Because, she was sure, he belonged there. That she was privileged to be his wife was all the glory Christine Five-coat could imagine existing for anyone.

She enjoyed her home, and managed it perfectly. It was always clean and beautiful. Serene. There were very few household crises in that home. And she also managed this primarily for the comfort and satisfaction of her husband. To anyone less than intimate, she spoke of him as "the doctor." To her friends, he was "dear Paul." To us children, he was "your dear father."

To us, he was indeed dear. So was our mother, and we were dear to each other. We really were. I, the oldest. Handsome Treadway, three years younger, and sturdy Alice Peck. In any other family she would have been a tomboy. But not in our home, of course, not a daughter of our mother, raising the children her husband had given her to raise properly.

Her husband, her home, her children were very important to Christine Peck Fivecoat, but above everything else in importance to her was my father's profession. That took precedence always. It was the main consideration in her life, and so it was in ours. We understood when Father could not attend a recital for which we had practiced for a year. Mother never grieved over a ruined soufflé because Father was delayed and late for dinner. "He had more important things on his mind."

If Father came home tired, the house and the children were kept quiet.

There was no altar to medicine in our home, but the reverence, the respectful awe was there. We were, our mother assured us, all privileged to have a doctor as the head of the house. We must help him as much as we could. It was a difficult profession. "Your dear father literally gives his life to the sick. Never forget that."

We did not forget it. Although the situation needed to be thought about. Tread sometimes tried to make a joke of it, but we girls were shocked at his attempt. We were too young to understand that a man could indeed "give his life" to his profession, yet have time to do all the other things which Father did and enjoyed. He seemed to live, and did live, a full life.

Which he shared with his family as fully as was possible. Attired in white tie and tails, Mother in brown chiffon with a Spanish shawl for a wrap, Father and Mother would depart for the Friday night symphony concert in the season, saying that they looked forward to the time when we would be able to go with them. It seemed a glamorous and worthwhile goal; I spent hours pretending that I was old enough, and going to the symphony.

We, all of us, lived a full life. In due time a TV set entered our home, but the programs were carefully chosen. Rock and roll, "I Love Lucy," and Sid Caesar, were not for us. A Tanglewood concert, the Telephone Hour, could be watched.

Father was the center of the home, but he included us all. I remember the tree house he had built in the branches of an old oak tree at the end of our garden. This was for Tread, who took no interest in it. He said he was afraid of falling, and perhaps he was. Alice and I liked it, though Alice was grounded after she persistently tried to climb ever higher in the tree, and eventually fell out of it, breaking her arm. But I was permitted to take my book up there — "with a sweater, darling, if it gets breezy."

I took the sweater, and longed for the breezes to come, to rise. I loved the sound they made in the thick leaves. I loved watching all the things to be seen from that height — which really was not very high, but did afford a view of the yard next door, and those of the homes behind us. Swimming pools, hula hoops, even bubble gum, were things forbidden to me, but I could get familiar with them as I sat reading in the tree house. I could hear the music of the record players and the radios, watch the dancing. Admiring one girl in particular because she had so much fun, and seemed so popular, I experimented with drawing my own soft blonde hair back into a pony tail, tying it with a ribbon. . . .

Mother caught me at it, and surveyed the result. "It's quite becoming, Joie," she told me. "Let me help . . ."

We went on trips, we attended concerts that were suitable, the Nutcracker at Christmas, a children's series given by the symphony on Sunday afternoons, but when I suggested that we might enjoy one of the light operas — I believe the current one was *Rosemarie* — being presented in the park, I met with gentle, but firm, denial.

I was looking at the newspaper. "The dancing would be lovely," I argued.

"You'll be taken to the theater when you are old enough," Father assured me. "And to the ballet as well."

I was pretty sure the ballet was different from a light opera or a musical comedy.

Father deplored the Korean War. "Of course it's a war!" he would declare. "No matter what you call it! And we'll go through all the inconveniences again. You'll see."

He was convinced that travel would be curtailed, so he bought a large globe and set it up in the library. At regular intervals we all would take a "trip" by way of that globe. I realize now the enormous amount of work he must have put into those trips. We would go to Switzerland, he would say. So there would be pictures, models even, of the ocean liner that would take us across the Atlantic. His fine forefinger would trace the course, with a few words about the southern route because of the danger of icebergs in the spring or even early summer. He explained about the *Titanic*.

"I'm sure glad," said little Alice Peck, "that we're only pertendin'."

Mother gently reminded her that the word "sure" was unnecessary, and that *pretend* could be found in the dictionary, *pertend* could not be.

"Okay," said Alice Peck. "When do we . . ."

"We don't say okay, Alice dear."

Father waited patiently. I knew the day was coming when Alice would ask why not. It wasn't that Saturday.

That Saturday we went to Switzerland. We learned to pronounce Gstaad. We shivered over the Alps, and the people who climbed them. Father showed us skis, and the boots — we were shown Alpine flowers, and a record of yodeling was played. We ended the day with Father wearing a hat with a chamois brush in its band; we girls had full skirts and embroidered aprons. Tread had an alpenstock, knee socks, and leather shorts. Our supper featured cheese and some delicious cookies.

The war had not prevented our going to Switzerland. Father was determined that this one would not touch us in any way, certainly its ugliness would be kept from us.

Though of course we were aware of it. In the newspaper, at school — but his efforts paid off because the result for us was an awakening of patriotism, a receptive air toward heroes. And otherwise our lives went along as planned. We attended dancing school, advancing according to our ages. We were given riding lessons, and Alice Peck became a horse, to Mother's dismay.

"Don't worry," said Father. "A lot of girls go through that stage."

"What can we do? Maybe a psychiatrist, Paul dear?"

"I don't think one will be needed."

"But — she *prances!*"

Father smiled and kissed Mother's cheek. "She wasn't very pretty either when she lost her baby teeth."

"You mean it's all a part of growing up?"

"Yes, dear."

"I wish they need not."

26

"You would be greatly distressed if they didn't, my sweet."

We were "growing up." As were our schoolmates, who talked about it.

I think my father regretted that he could not have a governess and tutor for us, and keep us safely at home, safe from what we might learn beyond the school subjects which he conceded to be necessary.

But we each one attended the "Girls" kindergarten, and then I entered the private Catholic school for girls which was near our home. In due time, Alice Peck did the same. The idea of co-education never entered our parents' mind. Tread enrolled in the boys' school, similar if not identical with my own. We were not of the Catholic faith, but these two schools, the Academy and the Hall, were considered to be safer than nondenominational schools. More disciplined, more conservative. Public schools were not considered at all. Our schools were close to our home. A maid could accompany us, sometimes our mother did, and by the time Tread was old enough to rebel against the escort, he was eligible to enter the "military school," also Catholic, and was transported by bus. He went there for nine years, and my parents considered it a good school.

Attending such institutions did not bother

us children. So far as we knew, all school-teachers smelled of Ivory soap and candle-wax, and wore black habits, long veils, and a starched linen wimple.

Our education could be considered good. We learned good manners, and good penmanship. Alice Peck and I hated the uniforms required of the Cathedral Academy girls. Dark blue pleated skirts of a dowdy length, and middy blouses which were exchanged for round-collared white ones when I was in the eighth grade. We hated them, too, and at home said something about the uniforms.

But since we never quarreled, the only comment was that "Joey is unhappy about the new school uniforms."

Just as Tread had got nowhere about the crew cut he was required to have when he entered the Brothers' College. His hair was brown, with a soft wave — I greatly envied him his hair. But to go with his two-tone blue uniform, the red stripes and all the gold insigne, he must have a severely short haircut. This necessity was carefully and kindly explained to him and to Mother.

Once explained, such subjects were never mentioned again. We could not whine, nor complain, just as we could not bring home any sort of tales that could be construed as gossip. We might say that one of our school-mates was living at the Academy for a time, but the matter of her parents' divorce was not to be mentioned. If it was mentioned, no one heard.

Really, as I tell of these things, I realize what an amazing insulation we were given against life. And yet my father was a doctor; he had studied and specialized in that most earthy part of the human body, the gut. I knew that, at the time. Much later I was to recognize the irony of the fact.

From the time I could think at all, and I suppose that was soon after Tread was born, I wanted to be a boy. As the years came along, I wanted to be a doctor. The first ambition was met with a smile, the second with a firm, "No, dear. Your brother should be the one."

But Tread didn't want any part of medicine. He was a bookish boy, very handsome — beautiful, even — and he had lovely manners.

Alice Peck, our little sister, was a darling child. Sturdy, athletic, with no nonsense about her. We all truly loved Alice.

And me. I wanted to become a doctor. My first step toward that career, my first ambition, was to go to Father's office. It was only across the street. . . .

Of course that street was a wide one. A boulevard, with a center parkway of green grass, flower beds, and trees. But one could see the windows of the Medical Arts Building from our windows, and I began to ask, and kept asking, to see Father's office. This was one point from which I was not gently dissuaded.

I was told, "It's no place for children, dear." When I repeated my request, I was told, "Your dear father is a very busy man."

This did not convince me. I knew that Philip, Alan, and Cynthia often went to Uncle Doc's office. They told how the nurses gave them stick candy, and sometimes took them to Knaup's for strawberry sodas. I never had a soda until I was in the Upper School.

But I eventually did get to see Father's office. I was twelve or thirteen. That was after Alice Peck broke her arm falling out of the oak tree. Uncle Doc took care of her, she was in the hospital for several days, came home with a cast, and was watched most carefully. A couple of times she went over to the office to have X-rays. I tried to make her tell me what it was like, but she didn't give me a very satisfactory report.

No, she had not been taken to Knaup's.

No, an X-ray didn't hurt.

Of course not! She was entirely nonchalant.

But then time came for the cast to be removed. "To be cut off." I think the word *cut* was what frightened her. Because she was frightened, and begged me to go with her, begged Mother and Father to let me go.

"Nonsense!" said Father.

"It would be too hard on Joey," said Mother.

But I spoke right up. "I'd be *glad* to go!" And I would be. I was glad at the prospect, though prudence made me try hard to conceal my eagerness.

So we went to Uncle Doc's office, which amounted to going to Father's. I can see our little group yet. It was summertime, about four in the afternoon. Mother wore a hat. She never went on the street without hat and gloves. Her hat that day was blue, to match her blue linen dress. My dress and Alice Peck's had been made by the ladies who sewed for the Women's Exchange. Alice's was green, sleeveless, with pleats in the skirt. Her curly yellow hair was tied back with a green ribbon. She wore white socks and Mary Janes. My dress was white, piped in red, and I wore red shoes, which I loved. I had agonized over whether I would tie my hair with a red or a white ribbon.

We walked out of the house, down the two flights of steps, then down along the sidewalk to the corner, where we waited for the traffic to be in our favor. We crossed over, went past the hotel's side entrance, past the garage and driveway . . .

"One must be very careful here," said Mother. Then past the shop window — the fur store had a stuffed mink in the window. Alice Peck must stop and talk to it. I liked the books set out in the next store, but I didn't linger. Because, just beyond, was the entrance to the Medical Building. There was gold lettering on black glass, heavy doors to open and go through. The lobby was tile-floored, and a smiling black man called my mother by name, and Alice Peck . . .

"They're going to cut off my cast!" she told him.

"This is our daughter, Joie," said Mother.

"Why, she's a real young lady!" His teeth flashed in a wide smile.

"Yes, Benny," said Mother. "I'm afraid she is, almost."

He took us up to the third floor, and told Alice Peck not to be afraid. "Doctah Winter, he never hurt any little girl!"

As we had been trained, Mother left the elevator first; we followed, and I stopped dead, right there. For on the opposite wall of the hallway there was a polished wooden plaque. Fastened to it were brown letters, also of wood, but darker.

I read the words aloud. "Purgers and Sawyers," they said, with Uncle Doc's name and Father's below them.

I frowned and looked at Mother.

"They just mean doctors," said Mother. "Physicians and surgeons."

Yes. I had seen the *Physician and Surgeon* bit down on the black glass.

"Come along, Joie," said Mother. "We mustn't keep a busy man waiting."

Alice Peck tucked her hand into mine, and together we did "come along." But the wheels were spinning in my head, and every sense was working overtime. I was so excited that I could hardly breathe. "Purgers and Sawyers," I kept repeating below my breath.

First we went into the waiting room, a rather large place with a few people seated there. The furniture was plain — wooden-framed chairs with leather cushions. There was a dark green rug on the floor, and some of Uncle Doc's paintings on the wall. I recognized the one of the barn at his home.

At the far side of the room was a glass window that looked through to where two women, one of them in a white uniform, sat at desks. One was using the typewriter. Mother went to the window and pushed its sliding glass open enough that she could be heard when she said, "We're here, Miss Belden."

Miss Belden jumped right up. "Come on back, Mrs. Fivecoat," she said. Miss Belden had very red hair.

We went through a door at the corner of the room, to a truly mysterious place of halls, doors, small rooms, and a brightly shining room full of glass and lights and fascinating sounds and smells. I could have stood right there and *looked* at what I knew was a laboratory.

But just then Father popped out of one of the doors; he looked rather different in a white jacket which wasn't at all like the white woolen one he wore to parties. There was a stethoscope around his neck, and his eyeglasses seemed to shine very brightly.

He was lovely to us, welcomed his "beautiful girls," and introduced me to people whom Alice Peck and Mother already knew.

He suggested that Mother and I might want to wait outside.

Alice nearly pulled my hand off. I was looking through the door at a cabinet full of shining instruments, and Father was laughing and saying, "Well, all right, then."

34

Then Uncle Doc came down the hall, looking bigger than ever in a long white gown, or apron, which tied behind his neck and around his waist. He spoke to Mother. "Christine, my dear . . ."

He flipped my pony tail and asked Alice Peck why she was holding my hand so tightly.

"Joey won't let you hurt me," said Alice Peck.

This startled me.

"Won't you, Joey?" asked Uncle Doc.

I shook my head. "I know you won't hurt her."

He smiled. "That's right, I won't. So you and your mother . . ."

Mother left, but Alice still clung to my hand, and she was shaking. So I went right along behind Uncle Doc. Father had disappeared. And I sat on a stool while Uncle Doc lifted Alice Peck to the table, and the nurse brought up the little cart with the instruments, among them the electric saw. "This will screech," said Uncle Doc, showing us that it would.

"Screeches don't hurt," I said. So Alice Peck kept looking at me, and I looked at her. I suppose my eyes were as big as hers. And the saw bit into the cast, and my head tingled — but I had never been happier in my life!

For there was Alice Peck's arm, all healed. It looked a little white, and maybe thin . . .

Uncle Doc kept doing things for Alice Peck, rubbing her arm, asking her to move her fingers and bend the elbow. And all the time, he kept talking to me, too. I could look around, he said. "Don't open any closed doors."

So I did explore, not touching a thing, but looking at the instruments on his cart, and going down the hall to stare, and stare, at the laboratory. I loved the way it smelled. When I came back, I told Uncle Doc that I was going to be a doctor.

"Are you, now?" he asked me. "What specialty will you follow?"

"I'm not joking."

"I hope you're not. If you plan to be a doctor. That's serious business."

"I know it is. Uncle Doc . . . ?"

He turned his head to smile at me. His eyes were very blue behind his dark-rimmed glasses. "Yes, Joey," he said kindly.

And I loved him, because I first realized then that I always had been able to ask him questions, knowing that he would give me the same sort of answer that he would give an adult.

"I want to ask you about that sign opposite the elevator," I told him. "The one that says you and Father . . ."

"Are purgers and sawyers," he completed my sentence. He was laughing, down in his throat. "Did you like that sign, Joey?"

"Oh, yes, sir, I think so. I didn't entirely *understand* it. . . ."

He nodded and lifted Alice Peck down from the table.

"Well, I'll tell you," he said. "Some time ago I saw an item in the newspaper of a medical meeting that was to be held right here in our city. That was way back in eighteen seventy-three. It said there would be a gathering of the — I'm quoting — *of the most eminent purgers and sawyers of the world.*"

"And you . . . ?"

"Yes. I told your dad — we were getting these offices set up at the time. I told him that was our sign. Our mark. He was the purger, of course. And" — his hand touched the electric saw — "you know what my profession is!"

I was delighted. "I suppose everyone asks about it?"

"Well, almost everyone. I think the names are good, don't you?"

I did.

I liked everything about Uncle Doc. He was my father's closest friend, as well as his medical associate, but I don't suppose two men could have been more different. Uncle Doc was older than Father. After military service he came back to the city to serve a residency in the same hospital where Father was also a resident.

Uncle Doc was a big man, a hearty man. I never heard him criticize the way our parents were raising us children. In those days he contented himself with showing us that there were other ways of life.

I was entirely happy in my home, and I dearly loved my parents. I appreciated their devotion to us.

But I loved Uncle Doc, too. I think we all did, though perhaps to varying degrees. Alice Peck could become almost hysterical at the prospect of a Saturday out at the Village.

To her this meant a chance to race and run, to ride one of the horses, and feed any or all of them. As I grew older, I began to inquire about this rural settlement that existed like a sheltered, living spring in the center of what was becoming a very busy suburban district. So, as had always been my, often deplored, custom, I asked questions. Philip became interested because I was, and together we pieced out facts about the Village as we knew it, and as it had become established.

I wrote down every detail in an old school

notebook which I no longer have, of course, but having written these things down, I remember them.

The Village had seventeen houses, and one hundred and ten acres of land. It still lies serenely to the south of one of the busiest highways in the county. No gasoline stations, apartment houses, or middle-income houses were ever allowed there.

At the time I asked, and excluding live-in help, the population numbered sixty-five, not counting dogs, either, or cats, horses, and assorted pets. The Village was conceived and built to be the perfect town, and it has continued to be that, governed by the wives of the friends, and friends of friends, who live in the community.

There were tall, wrought-iron entrance gates, and behind them a single, tree-lined street which branched into an oversize circular driveway.

Around this were scattered houses of brick and oak and stone, to create what Uncle Doc called artificial antiquity. Each house and owner possessed no more than two and a half acres of ground, the lawns carefully uncultivated, looking more like recently mowed hayfields than anything else.

Anyone buying into, and living in, the Village was most carefully screened by the governing committee of ladies.

The charm of the Village — spacious houses, sweeping lawns, barns, and even a purely decorative windmill — had been preserved by the enforcement of strict zoning and building ordinances. One time when our family was entertained by the squire of an estate in England, I felt quite at home in the same familiar atmosphere of gracious rural living as I had known in the Village.

The group of socially close people who first conceived the Village were almost immediately incorporated as a town, and a committee of the women became the trustees. They passed on all sorts of matters, and there was one time when a newly accepted resident presented five different plans for the home he wanted to build. The committee would accept nothing in the way of "modern" architecture, and the acreage purchased remained vacant. It still may be unused.

The original group were close friends, and practically lived in each other's homes. They shared parties, picnics, weddings and funerals. Naturally the younger generation diluted this close accord. As the old guard died or moved away, some of the strict rules were relaxed. The monthly town meeting no longer was a cocktail party with ordinances passed along with the hors d'oeuvres, though the townhall had continued to be the home of the Mayor. The "perfect town," as originally established, could not remain perfect for long. The bridle path was curtailed by the building of a new highway, and the horse population dropped from twenty to a single mare and a foal.

But when we knew it, the Village seemed entirely "perfect"; we enjoyed the privilege of visiting Uncle Doc there. His home was a large one, with a barn and other fascinating outbuildings. I believe he had established that home with the hope and plan of marriage. Some tragedy — never spoken of — destroyed those plans. Uncle Doc himself never mentioned the family he himself did not have. He maintained his home and cultivated his garden — only now can I realize what a wonderful garden it was. The neatness of the rows of beans, lettuce, cabbages — eggplant, tomatoes and okra — he raised every vegetable. There were fruit trees, and a strawberry bed. Currant bushes and raspberry vines . . .

Only now do I realize all the facets of this remarkable man. As a child I knew he was a doctor, that he was a specialist in bones, I knew he had his home where he could pick his own strawberries to add to the shortcakes he himself made. . . .

Now I know that, even when I first knew him, he was one of the leading orthopedists in the country. Now he is Chief of Orthopedic Surgery at the University Hospital Group, and chairman of the Department of Orthopedic Surgery at the University Medical School. When I was a child eavesdropping on the medical talk between Uncle Doc and my father, I learned of the way in which Uncle Doc had first achieved the healing of broken bones by the use of medullary pins, a technique developed in Nazi Germany, and, during the war, brought dramatically to the attention of army surgeons like Uncle Doc when former prisoners showed up with well-healed broken legs that had been cared for by the German surgeons. Bones had healed to walking capability within two months rather than the usual six. Healed with good, sound bony callus. X-ray examination showed the finger-thick metallic rods, or spikes, which extended down through the medulla, or canals of upper leg bones from hip to knee, like ramrods run through gun barrels. I was especially intrigued with that simile. Since then men like Uncle Doc have used these pins, developing them, in the treatment of broken legs, arms, shoulders and fingers, in the plastic surgery of deformed legs, and in the control of bone diseases.

But he still claimed that the technique was the greatest German contribution to medicine since the use of sulfa drugs.

He shared, as I have told, offices with my father, and as I grew older, I came to know something of the work he did, particularly in rehabilitating the injured or diseased. He called the patients "children," no matter their age; I became fascinated by the means he used to restore mobility and use to crippled limbs.

Uncle Doc — I overheard the beginning of this discussion, too, though later the matter was discussed rather openly between him and my parents — Uncle Doc wanted Father to move his family out to the Village. Some acreage had become available through a death, and a house was already built. I was ecstatic at the idea, as were Tread and Alice Peck — Alice more noisily so than Tread. But Father decided against making any move. He was a city boy, he argued, and liked being able to walk to his office and to the hospital where he, too, was on the staff and taught in the medical school.

Father did belong to the University Club, as Uncle Doc did, but it was Uncle Doc who always came for us children on Easter morning to hunt for gilded eggs tucked into the crevices of the Club's luxurious leather chairs. Philip always gave me the eggs he found, a practice which infuriated Alice Peck. "It's because you're a girl!" she told me.

"Well, of course I am. If you'd be nice to Alan, he might give you his eggs."

"I'd rather find my own."

And she did find them, sometimes showing up with more in her basket than I did.

Uncle Doc's niece and nephews lived with their widowed mother in the Village. Their house was not as big as Uncle Doc's, but it was a pleasant place. It was built of brick, painted white, with a lot of porches, and inside there were large square rooms. Mrs. Daly worked somewhere in the city, I never did know just where. I always got the impression that Father did not like her. Or maybe he didn't like her staying on in the Village. I don't believe he saw much of her. She was a slender woman, with light red hair drawn firmly back into a knot. If she were at home when we'd go into the house, she would give us hot chocolate and delicious coconut toast, a matter of soaking bread strips in milk, sprinkling them with coconut and sugar, and baking them in the oven. I've never met up with coconut toast anywhere else. As I grew older, I entertained the idea that Uncle Doc should marry Mrs. Daly, but when I spoke of it, both my mother and father told me not to be foolish, though the idea still sounded good to me. Uncle Doc called his sister-in-law "Stel," and they seemed to like each other. Her children were about the same age as we were — Philip six months older than me, Cynthia two years older than Alice Peck, with Alan coming along in between.

They attended the Country Day school, and we girls came to wish that we could go there, too. Everyone seemed to have more fun, there were teams and archery contests and such events. The Winter "kids" — we couldn't use that term at home — learned to care for and ride Uncle Doc's two horses, and they could do it — ride, I mean — whenever they wished. I envied them. And I liked them, too, until we grew older and Philip began to get what Alice Peck called "mushy" about me.

"Propinquity," my father explained this development to my mother. "Dick throws the children together too much, perhaps."

This explanation deflated my ego. I had thought maybe I was getting to be attractive to boys. And I was really upset when I realized that we weren't going out to the Village as much as we had been doing. I told Uncle Doc how much I missed those trips.

"What happened?" he asked me.

"Father calls it propinquity," I said, in what may have been my first evidence of disloyalty or criticism of my father.

Uncle Doc got pink all over his face and bald spot. Maybe he said something to Father. Maybe he just made more special efforts to invite us out to the Village. And after that I tried to prevent Phillp's being "mushy."

"Our parents would like it better if we were all friends together," I told him. He seemed to understand, and that's the way we were — for several years.

By then I was fourteen, and I was finding it pleasant to talk to boys. I wished more than ever that we could go to Country Day school, which was co-educational. I did enjoy it when we went to their football games, and to the spring horse show. Alice Peck and I used to talk about it, and wondered why our parents so insisted on the Cathedral schools with their prim ideas about segregation of the sexes. Tread didn't join us in our frustration. The one time we included him in such a conversation he assured us that girls were silly; he was glad he did go to a boys' school.

"He's talking about sisters," I assured Alice Peck.

When I mentioned changing schools to Uncle Doc, he said it was a good idea, but not one "your father would entertain, Joey."

Right then I wanted to ask him, I should have asked him, how he and my father, so different in so many ways, could be such good friends. When I was fourteen, he would have answered me; he would have given me an adult reply which would take the years of thinking about that I needed for full understanding.

But I didn't ask him, and later . . .

They were different, and in so many ways. Tastes, ideas about social things, about the clothes to wear, church services and table manners. And yet they were the closest of friends. Professionally, of course, but their relationship went much deeper than that. I first guessed that Father leaned on Uncle Doc; it was only when trouble came that I realized how much Uncle Doc needed my father.

They agreed on many things, especially professional matters, but they could argue hotly about such things, too.

I especially remember one time when my father had a little malpractice trouble.

Oh, not really. Not malpractice. But it came close enough that I at least was very frightened. Father and Uncle Doc argued for years about that case, so I pretty well know what happened.

We were on vacation, and had rented a cottage on the Maine coast. We sometimes did this sort of thing, taking our cook along as general manager of the household. She had been with us for years, and we children loved her and obeyed her as well.

That particular evening Temperance was going to help us cook our supper out on the beach. I don't remember anything about the meal except that I am sure we enjoyed it. I loved the ocean. Father and Mother were driving to a resort twenty-five miles away, and would have their dinner at the hotel there.

They did this, Father a little annoyed to find that a convention was being held at the hotel, and the annual banquet was going on at the end of the same dining room. Not a large convention, nor a large dinner, I believe. It was a Lodge gathering, I think Father told afterward.

At any rate, of course lobster was featured, and in the course of the meal, one man rose from his chair, took two steps, and collapsed. Father had been looking that way, and was instantly at his side, kneeling beside him. He pronounced the man dead, and said someone should send for the coroner.

This official turned out to be the local undertaker, and his first remark was to the effect that "Jim's old ticker finally gave out on him."

Father agreed that things looked as if it had. The restaurant owner, a friend of Jim's, confirmed that Jim's heart had been bad for years. A bottle of nitroglycerin tablets was found in Jim's pocket.

The coroner asked Father to give him a statement that the victim had died of a heart attack.

"I'd rather wait for the autopsy," said Father.

"But . . ." said the coroner. Father told the story word for word to Uncle Doc, and later discussion made me feel as if I'd been present.

"But," said the coroner, "autopsies cost the taxpayer money, and they make things hard for the kinfolk. I'd like to save Jim's widow that. So if you could give me a statement . . ."

Here's where Uncle Doc said Father made a mistake. He finally had agreed to give the man his statement, which Jim's widow did not appreciate one bit. She insisted on an autopsy, which revealed that there had been no coronary thrombosis. Jim had choked to death on a large, poorly masticated bolus of lobster which had lodged in his larynx.

The widow collected double indemnity, and fortunately did not sue Father for malpractice.

"She could have done so!" Uncle Doc insisted, and many times. "And any trial would have made you look mighty foolish, Paul."

"I'll never again reveal my professional status in public," said Father glumly.

"Nor play the Good Samaritan, I suppose?" asked Uncle Doc.

"Certainly not!"

Sometimes the conversation ended there, sometimes Uncle Doc would go off into a discussion of coroners and medical examiners. One of the latter, he claimed, would have known that choking at a banquet can often be misdiagnosed as a coronary occlusion.

"One might say that a medical examiner was present," said Father stiffly.

"You're a competent physician, but how many deaths from unknown causes come under your hands?"

"You mean I lack the proper experience."

"Oh, Paul, don't be an ass! I mean, a medical examiner sees these things. You don't, very often."

"And the medical examiner . . ."

"In place of an undertaker-coroner, yes.

He would have ordered the autopsy."

"You think."

"Well, sure, I think. I know that some medical examiners can botch things. And that all coroners don't. Some of them keep that outdated name, but work strictly within a model medico-legal system."

I always hoped this last big word would be explained for me; the dictionary didn't help much. And after that particular case, lobster, even the coast of Maine, became tricky subjects for Father. I think he took Uncle Doc's advice on such matters, but if he ever acknowledged that he did — I wouldn't know.

Father and Uncle Doc frequently had disputes on other matters. For one, they could argue about their membership in the University Club, and do it frequently. I don't remember that particular discussion, but it was revealed that Uncle Doc had argued Father into joining the Club in the first place.

Every time something would happen to displease Father, or some decision was made contrary to his liking, they would have an argument.

"You're not going to like this, Paul," Uncle Doc would say, "but the board has decided to let women eat Sunday breakfast in the grill."

Father did not like that decision. A male club should be just that. "We need a new board," he would mumble.

I believe that he resented the fact that Uncle Doc was on that board, while he was not. Though he was the most formal of men, he said sarcastic things about the board meetings.

"A black-tie affair, always, Christine," he would explain to my mother. "Dick, of course, has to get someone to tie his black one. He's never learned how."

Mother would smile gently at Uncle Doc, and put her hand on Father's sleeve.

Chapter 2

As the years passed and we children grew older, our relationships with each other changed, too. Our relations with the Winter children. Philip got tall very quickly, and his voice changed. He also became really interested in me. He would stick as close to me as he could whenever we'd be out at the Village, or when Uncle Doc took us to some athletic event at the Country Day school. For a very brief period Uncle Doc teased me about Philip's "crush," but something made him stop. Perhaps Father or Mother said something, perhaps I showed my lack of interest in Philip. I really liked Alan much better. He was a little younger than I was, Philip a little older. Both boys had red hair, but Alan was more handsome. Cynthia, their sister, was dark.

Philip liked to take walks, and wanted to hold hands with me. He liked to sit beside the Village pond and talk about books. Alan was interested in sports — any kind of sports. With Alan, a girl had to be good at baseball or tennis — he was not interested in her at all as a girl.

If she could pitch straight, or serve a proper tennis ball, he would tolerate her.

Since I was only fair at such things, he liked Alice much better than he did me. Alice was about four years younger, but she could beat him at tennis, and do it every time. I remember the way Mother lectured Alice Peck about this. Girls should not beat boys at games, she insisted.

"You mean Alan?"

"I mean any girls and any boys, dear," said Mother.

"You mean Alan. He's the one I beat most. But, Mother, he taught me to play tennis, why wouldn't he want me to beat him? Just tell me *why?*"

Mother glanced at me. "You know, don't you, Joey?"

I thought I did, but I wouldn't be able to say that her reasons had to do with our debuts, and later our weddings.

Mother had begun to plan those affairs the day Alice Peck and I were born. Whenever we took a trip to Europe, she bought linens for our trousseaux. She inspected every freckle-faced boy who came to our birthday parties as a prospective or impossible bridegroom.

I didn't know about Tread, but Alice Peck

and I did not like Cynthia Winter as well as we did her brothers. And I don't believe that feeling had much to do with her being a girl, as we were.

Of course, being a girl, she was always grouped with Alice Peck and me. She was the youngest of the Winters, but she still was only a year younger than Tread. That put her four years younger than me, but she always seemed much older in her ways and in her interests. Alice Peck and I did not like her, but we knew we shouldn't show it, or speak of our feeling.

Our dislike had nothing to do with the different way the Fivecoats had been raised from the Winter children — nor the fact that we liked different things.

It had a great deal to do with the fact that Cynthia was boy-crazy. Crazy about any boy, or boys. She liked to talk about them; she would make big eyes at the gardener's boy out at the Village, or smile at some boy in the restaurant where Mother took us girls for luncheon. Later she would tell us that the gardener's boy had "got fresh" with her, or that the boy in the restaurant had made his parents sit at the next table so he could watch Cynthia. She would toss her long black hair, and prim her lips. "I don't need to depend on pick-ups," she would tell us.

Alice Peck and I knew the truth about each encounter, but we did not venture to argue with Cynthia, and certainly we did not mention the matter to Mother. Cynthia also had soft, beguiling ways with all grown-ups. She could fool even Uncle Doc. Temperance said "Butter wouldn't melt in Miss Cynthia's mouth when she wants somethin'."

Alice Peck and I knew what she meant. We weren't supposed not to like people, and we didn't say much to each other even about Cynthia, but we had an understanding on the subject.

This didn't bother Cynthia one bit. She went right on being both silly and curious about boys, about sex. She told us things, and asked questions.

Alice Peck did ask me once why we should have to be with her.

"I suppose we have to take Cynthia if we go out to the Village and see very much of Uncle Doc," I told my little sister.

She nodded. We both were acknowledging that we could not, possibly, give up Uncle Doc.

And so our childhood passed, happily and safely. Each day was much the same as the days before, and as the days ahead would be. A few things changed. We children were getting older, for one. Alice Peck and I were offered our own bedrooms, and Alice looked fearfully at me, knowing that the decision would be mine.

But I shook my head. "I'd miss Alice," I said. "Though maybe the rabbits . . ."

Everyone laughed. And our large bedroom was redecorated, the cute little bunnies were replaced by chintz-patterned wallpaper, and new maple beds and desks were purchased.

We knew we lived according to a fixed routine, but since the habits were pleasant, we enjoyed knowing what to do and to expect. We liked the trips Father planned and that we took. We liked the family picnics, the expeditions to the Art Museum and to the Botanical Gardens.

But best of all, especially best, we loved Christmas. We did not want a single thing ever changed about that. The red-ribbon-tied holly wreath on our white front door, the smaller ones in all the front windows of the house. The tall tree that was set up in the hall, and trimmed on Christmas Eve, Father leaning over the stair rail to affix the angel on the top. When Tread was twelve, he began saying that Tread was going to take over that job. But he never did.

Bright packages were brought out of hiding and heaped at the base of the tree. We children went to bed, and Father and Mother went to midnight service at the church, peeking in on us when they returned; we pretended to be asleep.

Christmas Day began early in the morning, with Father protesting loudly at being "routed out." We children were allowed to come downstairs in our robes and slippers, to spend an hour opening our gifts, exclaiming over them. Breakfast was served then — a very nice breakfast of fruit and thinly sliced ham, eggs, biscuits, and hot chocolate for the children.

Then we must dress quickly, and the whole family went to church, walking the three blocks unless there had been snow.

I remember the picture we must have made. Father in his dark blue topcoat and Homburg hat, Mother with a dark fur hat and a jacket to match. We children — Until I was sixteen, Alice Peck and I wore coats to match, sometimes navy, sometimes red. They were straight, unadorned woolen coats. Beneath them we wore simple dresses, because after church we would drive out to Uncle Doc's, and Mother admitted resignedly that things would be rowdy there.

They were not actually rowdy. There would be laughter, and voices raised in competition with other voices. A roaring fire in the big fireplace, and the never-to-be-forgotten Christmas smell of oranges and fresh popcorn, roasting turkey and the big evergreen tree.

We took gifts with us when we went out to the Village, and in return we children found Christmas stockings for us hung beside the fireplace. Philip and Alan and Cynthia had claimed theirs at "the crack of dawn." The stockings were of red felt with our names embroidered on them, and along with the orange and the big red apple, the nuts and the candies, there was always some gift we especially wanted. I got my first lipstick in my Christmas stocking.

My mother did not approve. "Oh, no!" she said softly.

"Joey's fifteen," Uncle Doc reminded her.

"I know. But I wish she wouldn't be — not yet."

I was allowed to keep the lipstick, and I used it discreetly enough that it was not mentioned again.

Christmas Day was noisy at Uncle Doc's. We played games, we square-danced — Mrs. Daly played the piano for us. We laughed a lot. An enormous dinner was served at four o'clock, but before it we — most of us — took a walk the length of the bridle path, at least — to get up an appetite.

Dinner was a wonderful affair, Uncle Doc happily presiding at the head of the table, carving the glistening brown turkey, laughing, telling funny stories of other Christmases. His housekeeper, cook, and houseman had done the work, but it was Uncle Doc's feast, all the way. I loved Christmas dinner at his house, the tall stack of plates at his hand, the way he wielded the huge carving knife. The cranberries, the bowls of potatoes and vegetables, handed around, oyster scallop and fried corn. The finale of the Christmas pudding, ablaze, which Uncle Doc carried triumphantly into the dining room and around the table.

"I don't know why we aren't all sick!" Mother would say as we were going home.

But we never were. Tired, sleepy, but always entirely content with Christmas Day, with the happy circle of love which had enclosed us all.

I don't believe Father and Mother were really snobbish about our activities and friendships. I think it was our friends and acquaintances who recognized, who respected us, as a closed circle, and helped to keep us that way.

Father and Mother conducted a fairly busy social life. We children gave little parties, especially for our birthdays, and we attended parties given by others. We each went to dancing school and attended the exclusive fortnightly dances — The Fortnightly — given by that school during the winter season. These were admitted to be the forerunner of the debut balls and the adult social affairs. Here we could demonstrate the manners which had been taught to us at dancing school and in our homes — or not, as the case might be.

In those years of hula hoops, strapless evening gowns, and black leather jackets, formality was being cherished and clutched at defensively.

I think that I was born interested in people. Mother used to sigh and say how different her children were, each from the other. Treadway was quiet, even shy. Alice Peck was everybody's friend, and everybody liked her. Joey — "She's curious, really. She watches people, and things that happen. As if she were keeping a record."

This was, indeed, very astute of my mother. I was interested in people, and in what people did. I began this interest in my home, I carried it with me wherever I went.

"Don't stare, Joey," became the most familiar of all words to me. And my reply: "I'm not staring, I'm looking."

What I looked at were people. The ones at home. Temperance, Hermann the houseman, and our nursemaid. My parents, my brother and sister. The people I saw on the streets, at school, at church, at the Club. All were fascinating.

Some I wanted to know better, and talk to. Mother and Father, even Uncle Doc, were kind, persuasive, then stern with Alice Peck and me. "Little girls must not talk to strangers, dear. Nor let them talk to you."

It was years before I understood why they should not, but a strict habit of obedience stood us in good stead.

But people who were not strangers — my schoolmates, for example — I knew them. Why shouldn't I bring even one of these girls home with me? If they wanted to come. Yes, I was forbidden to go anywhere but home after school, but other girls had more freedom.

And occasionally — not often, but occasionally — I would bring such a girl home with me. Mother was always lovely to my guests. We would be offered cookies and milk, we spent an hour out in the garden, or up in my room, talking, looking at things. Then Mother would ask Hermann to drive my guest home, with me going along.

Afterward, Mother would gently explain to me that she preferred to select my friends.

"Sally's a nice girl . . ." I would defend my visitor.

"She is a very nice girl, dear. When I know her better, as well as her mother, perhaps she would be a friend I would select."

I never broke over and went to see the girls I knew at school. Alice Peck did, and got into what she called "a heap of trouble" about it. She was supposed to return home at a fixed time, to walk the block or two, or ride the school bus. There were to be no deviations from this rule. "Are you going to make me walk to and from school with you, Alice?" asked Mother. "Or have Hermann take you?"

"I can't see . . ."

"I'll try to explain. Then, if you still cannot understand, you must accept this as a rule. We won't argue about it."

No. We never argued about anything. But Alice was not satisfied with the situation, and she asked me if I were.

"I'm waiting to grow up," I admitted.

"You'll do that lots sooner than I will, Joey."

"I know."

"Then I'll be all alone."

"You're feeling sorry for yourself."

And she giggled, then said that she wasn't. Not really. But she did think we might do some of the things that the other girls at school did, things that the Winter kids did. . . .

"Don't say 'kids,' Alice P."

She sighed. "I know. But they have fun. They don't get hurt. And they even ride the bus into the city to go to the library, and things."

I knew they did. I envied them.

After a few weeks, Alice and I included Tread in our talk. We asked him if he didn't wish he could do things on his own . . .

"What sort of things?" he asked.

"Oh, go for a sundae at Knaup's, or . . ."

"Chocolate makes my face break out."

It did.

"But don't you *ever* want to do *anything* outside of this house and family?" I asked.

"Why should I?"

"I don't know if you *should*, but wouldn't you like it?"

"I don't think so, Joey. I like the way Mother and Dad set things up for us. And personally I hope they keep on doing it. I'd stand ready to fight anybody who might want to change things."

"You'd better not fight me!" said Alice Peck darkly.

I laughed. To my knowledge, Tread Five-coat had never fought anything!

Alice Peck, almost from the first, did not stay within the closed circle. I knew this, and when she was about ten, or eleven maybe, she talked particularly to me about it. She also declared that she did not mean to stay within it.

"I'm me, Joey," she declared. "I want to be me. So I want to decide what I shall become. Maybe Grandpapa and Grandmamma told Father who he was to be, but I don't really believe they did. It's like Tread when he used to say we couldn't step on the grass between the stones in the garden. He said terrible things would happen. So I stepped on it, and nothing happened. Remember? How he used to pretend he was a soldier or a policeman, and try to force us . . . ?"

I remembered. Tread had patrolled the garden walk. Mother said it was a game of pretend, just as we girls pretended with our dolls.

Only Alice never played much with dolls. She'd rather have roller skates, she would announce before her birthday or Christmas.

I was startled to know how deeply she was rebelling against the family regime. I knew she had stepped on the grass. I had known that she was impulsive, and said things, did them, for which she was reproved. But she was so little — I defended her to myself. Though now — She was a smart child, read and talked, and performed in school, beyond her age level — what really startled me was to know that she had a mind of her own, and used it.

I let her talk to me as much as she wanted. There really wasn't any reason, she said, why we shouldn't wear white anklet socks — even the bulky, thick ones. She had swapped something for a pair, and changed to them after she got to school. They were permitted with the uniform, so they couldn't be bad.

I wished she wouldn't risk Mother's hurt disapproval, but I knew she was right, too. It would be better to look more like the other girls. I had been laughed at, and called names, for dressing and talking and doing as I did. I still had that happen. Now Alice Peck was going through the same thing.

Once when we were going to a concert, she rebelled against wearing the long-waisted, Swiss embroidered white dress — it matched mine except that her sash was pink and mine was blue. She rebelled to me, and when her dress turned up with a torn hem, I suspected strongly that this had been no accident.

"We look dumb," she told me when I

protested with her.

We did. Different, at any rate.

"They're A Apple Pie clothes," said Alice. She meant Kate Greenaway. "Don't you get tired of dressing like me, and always walking side by side with me when the family goes anywhere?"

I knew what she meant. Five years older, I was often forced to wear clothes too young for me.

"I don't want to look like you, Joey," Alice Peck would tell me earnestly. "I love you, but I'm *not* you, and never will be."

No. She never would be. She was right. Our parents should recognize her as an individual. I began to watch her more closely. This was not always easy, because there was that five-year gap in our ages. But I could do it some of the time. And I discovered that she really didn't subscribe to the family rules. We attended art lectures at the Museum together, and dancing class, though there we were separated into different age groups. Alice Peck never brought her art sketches home, I discovered, because she liked to go off and sketch things for herself. She was quite good and the teacher encouraged her. I don't know that my parents would have reproved her for the drawings she made of nude sculpture or the copies of Remington

Indians, but she didn't take any chances. Uncle Doc liked the way she drew and used color when we'd go out to the Village and she'd spend the day at his elbow while he painted the birch trees beside the pond.

"For the nine hundredth time," Father joked.

"They never look the same twice," said Uncle Doc.

"The trees, the pond, or your painting?"

Uncle Doc did not answer him. I decided that he often used the same means as did Alice Peck. He wouldn't approve, but he preferred not to stir up an argument. Arguments with Father could be bruising, he had found.

Alice may have only guessed this, but she was quietly going her way. Not doing anything dangerous, or even disgraceful, of course. But at parties she branched out quite a lot. She made her own friends, and went her own way. She had fun doing that, I am sure. When we'd return from some party, Mother would complain that Alice always came home disheveled, and sometimes even dirty. I knew it was because she had swung highest in the swings and had successfully claimed the most balloons. She scuffed her slippers and soiled her white silk socks by walking the brick edging of a flower bed and slipping off. She played with the household dog, and her hair ribbon came off. . . .

Of course I did not speak of these things to my parents, and I didn't talk about them to Alice Peck either. Somehow this became an ethical thing, though difficult. I knew she would go her own way, and I hoped it would be as wonderful as she expected it to be. For myself, I was glad that she was being reasonably careful, though sometimes my parents must have known that her foot had strayed out of line.

My own life was changing, and even greater changes were imminent. I did not want trouble about Alice to impose itself just then. I began going to parties without her. There were luncheons, and tennis parties . . . I asked Alice if she was hunt.

She looked surprised. "Not me!" she assured me. "Most of those parties are dumb, aren't they?"

I didn't know. They were the only parties I knew about. Our nursemaid no longer accompanied us, but we were just about as closely supervised.

Chapter 3

The next I knew, I was eighteen, and I went away to college. I don't know if I *wanted* to go or not. But the idea of going had always been a part of my life. And since I liked books, and even study, I expected to like college. I would have a roommate my own age, and I would be free to make certain decisions for myself. The prospect both pleased and worried me.

"You'll do fine," Uncle Doc assured me. "You like people, and you're a cute girl to look at. Just don't let anybody borrow your last sweater. You won't enjoy freezing to death. I sort of wished you would be going to our University . . ."

"But that's co-ed," I reminded him.

"You bet it is. You're not afraid of the boys, are you, Joey?"

"No. I never have been. But —"

"I know. Your parents don't like the idea of a co-ed school for their daughter."

Mother said it would take the bloom off. I had heard her say that. Alice laughed about the statement. "Does she really think girls have bloom any more?" she asked.

I felt sure that if any girls did have it, I would be one of them. "I call it ignorance," I mumbled into my pillow. Suddenly, I was frightened to death of this new experience.

I believe that my parents had long before determined on the college I would attend. They may even have enrolled my name, just as they had Tread's at Father's alma mater.

But the last year of high school was marked by trips with me so that I could look at various schools.

I could have been happy at any of them. I knew Alice would have selected the one in the southwest, with horses to ride, polo a possibility, and horse shows a big feature; the desert was beautiful, as were the red-tiled roofs of the white buildings.

I saw schools perched above the Pacific, colleges cool and green in the mountains of New England, beautiful and slow-paced in Virginia.

The one chosen was small. Girls rode bicycles, and braided their hair, were healthy, brown and friendly. Education was the big ploy there, and I was anxious to get about mine. One could learn to speak French by living in a house where only French was spoken at meals, and I could take courses in the big science building. "I plan to be a doctor," I told the registrar who showed us about.

My father laughed. "She's said that since she was eight," he explained.

I still meant it. Right then I realized that I should have made some effort toward attending the University at home.

At Christmas, when I came home for the three-week vacation, I made my debut into the city's society, as was expected of me, and of my parents. Mother gave a tea in our home to present me to her friends and those older. And then there was a dance at the University Club; Philip was my escort, and Treadway. Again there were quantities of flowers, and all the young people whom I had known since childhood. I wished that Alan could have been one of my official escorts; Philip always acted so possessive. More so than my own brother. Alan was there, of course, and so was Alice Peck. These younger kids had lots more fun than we older girls did, with our twenty-four-button gloves and carefully set hair. My dress was of white tulle, with a rose-colored satin sash. Mine was a "sweet" debut dance, not the big ball with queens and maids of honor, and all that. I was glad; I never could have walked the length of a big ballroom, with hundreds of people watching, and made any sort of bow when presented. No, my debut was a select affair, very nice, and very *blah.*

But I was out In society. I had thank-you notes to write, and decisions to make about accepting or refusing invitations to other parties.

"With Philip and Treadway," said Mother comfortably, "you won't have to worry about escorts."

"Alan's old enough, too, isn't he?" I asked.

"Yes. He is," said Mother.

I didn't have to worry about escorts and parties for very long because the vacation was soon over, and I was on my way back to school, meeting the group for my college at the airport.

"Just like summer camp," one of these girls giggled. "Where did you go, Joey?"

"I never went to camp. I was one of those under-privileged girls." I had learned to make this sort of reply, lightly.

The other girl stroked the sleeve of my beaver jacket. "I can tell," she drawled.

At the end of four years, I graduated, as expected. I had studied as much science as I could, as the college offered. My grades were good. But I went through the maypole routine, too, and the daisy chain bit.

That summer I was a bridesmaid at three different weddings. Well, in three different parts of the country! From place to place, taxi, planes, even a hotel, I was allowed to travel by myself, and I liked doing it. My classmates took that sort of thing as a matter of course. I did not. Such freedom was a big step for me.

The weddings were exciting, and Mother loved the flurry of long dresses, and dyed slippers to be unpacked. I must tell her every detail, even to the small, amusing bobbles — she smiled wistfully over the faded, crushed bouquets, and stroked the ribbons.

"Was this a pretty one, Joey?" she asked. "With the brown?"

"Oh, it really was quite a pink wedding, Mother. My dress was brown chiffon over pink satin, you know, and our brown hats had loads of pink roses on them. Yes, it was really a lovely wedding. I was the only short bridesmaid, so I walked alone, behind the flower girl. . . ."

Mother smiled, and nodded. "Before long," she told me, "we'll busily be planning your own wedding."

"Oh, Mother!"

"You'll see," she assured me.

"I still want to study medicine," I told her.

During my senior year I had determined to be quite firm about that. I was going to apply — Uncle Doc would help me if my father would not. Though I didn't see how he could refuse. . . .

That morning, Mother only smiled indulgently and said that I should leave such things to Philip, who already was in medical school, and of course to Treadway when his time came.

Tread was then a freshman in college, having lagged a year. His grades were not as good as were required for his college, and he'd gone to a tutoring school.

I was disappointed that Mother would not take me seriously, and when the subject came up again in Father's presence, I held stubbornly to my dream. I knew that I could do well in medicine.

"You can be a candy-striper, Joie," Mother told me firmly, going back to my real name, though for years she had settled on Joey.

"I am too old to be a candy-striper," I said, just as firmly.

Alice Peck, across the table, was watching Mother and me, her big eyes bright, her head turning from one of us to the other.

"You're twenty-one," my mother agreed. "I don't know about the age limits . . . ?"

She looked questioningly at Father.

"You could be an aide," he said. "Not on the floor, of course."

"Why not?" I asked, feeling a rising sense of panic. *Could* they refuse me? Did it mean I would never study medicine?

"Aides do the dirty work," said Alice Peck, lifting her water goblet so she could hide behind it.

Father stared at her. "What do you know about aides?" he asked politely, but coldly, too.

"I've been in the hospital."

"When was this?"

"When she broke her arm, Paul," said Mother, smiling.

"Good heavens! I had completely forgotten. I knew that we were never steady patrons of the hospital's services."

"You keep us too healthy," said Mother sweetly.

And the matter of my being an aide, or of studying medicine, became lost for that evening.

But there was always Uncle Doc. The next time I saw him — we went out to the Village for Fourth of July — I explained my problem.

"Have you applied?" Uncle Doc asked me.

"I know that I should have, but —"

"Well, of course you counted on help from your father and me."

"Yes, I did. But — why couldn't I study medicine?"

"Well, Joey — I suppose you could. We take in a few girls at the school, and they seem to do all right."

"I made good grades at college. But Father and Mother . . ."

"Are they still worrying about your losing that bloom?" His eyes twinkled at me.

I laughed. "I suppose they are. And Mother is planning on my wedding as my next adventure. Though there isn't a man in sight."

"Young men are not what they were in my day."

"Are you going to change the subject, too, Uncle Doc?"

He looked shocked. "Of course I'm not! Let's see. You want to study medicine, but your parents refuse to let you. Pay the tuition for one thing."

"They disapprove, yes. Mother suggested I be a hospital aide, but Father didn't much like the idea."

"Well, we have some Junior League girls working for us. As Volunteers, you know. They seem to enjoy it, and are a real help. Why don't you ask the personnel office,

Joey? There surely is something you could do. You might even get paid for it."

"And I could save my money and enter medical school ten years from now."

He looked sorry. "You could make an issue of it right now," he reminded me.

"I know. But I haven't the strength to go against their wishes. Alice Peck, maybe. Not me."

"Your brother uses other means — or does he?"

"Boys are different."

He chuckled. "Yes, they surely are. Well, maybe the best I can offer is to stand behind you, Joey dear."

I nodded. "I know you'll do that, Uncle Doc. And I'll think of some way . . ."

"You are unhappy about this medical thing, aren't you?"

"Yes. Father could be right. I might not do well. But I would like to try."

Now I can realize how deeply I resented not being allowed to study medicine. I had spent four years of college work preparing to do just that, only to be gently, lovingly, firmly refused.

To be so thwarted was not to be endured! I told myself this. And if it *was* endured . . .

In a spirit of stiff hurt, of bitter disappointment. I decided to be the daughter of the house my parents claimed to want me to be.

They would give the orders. They would furnish me a home. They would support me. They wanted me to be meekly obedient. And so I would be. I wrote out specific resolutions to govern my behavior.

Of course, before very long, I relaxed, and did more than seem to accept their dictum.

As I recognized that I was being sorry for myself, things began to change for me. I still acknowledged the support and shelter arguments as valid, but I let something of myself emerge from the fog.

By September, I found some acceptable work to do at the hospital center. I worked in the library of the medical school, and was promised that I would also be assigned to the patients' library. Would I be strong enough to handle the heavy book cart?

"I'm small," I answered, "but I'm strong enough."

In the school library, I often saw Philip, and when I would agree to go with him for coffee, or even when I would agree to have a date with him, I made him talk about medical school. I don't think he preferred that subject, but being around the students had increased rather than appeased my unhappiness about not entering the school myself. I looked critically at the women students, and decided in all cases that I could do as well as any of them. I questioned some of the girls, trying to find how they had managed.

One was studying medicine because her father was a doctor and wanted her to follow his profession.

"Don't you like it?"

She shrugged.

"I envy you," I told her.

"But isn't your father a doctor?"

"Yes, but he doesn't think I should be one."

"You can do it anyway."

I didn't think I could. If I were Alice Peck, I might. She managed to do the things she wanted to do. For instance, she had been driving a car since she was sixteen. That summer I, too, learned, but it was not quite the same.

At twenty-one, I was expected to learn to drive. With Alice — I watched her, and tried to decide just how she managed to do pretty well as she wanted to do, all the time seeming to stay within the family standards and their approved limits.

I loved my parents and wanted to please them, but there were times when I felt I might be allowed more freedom than they seemed pleased to give me.

Watching Alice, I did learn to do a few things without asking for, or getting, my parents' approval. I wouldn't, of course, do anything extreme. I had standards of my own.

But there were things — well, like wanting to observe my father when he performed surgery. Within a few months, delivering books around the hospitals, I had become familiar with the complex's layout, and also ethical behavior, so I knew what would be possible. I had learned not to speak of such desires to my parents. Once I would be specifically forbidden to sit in the o.r. amphitheater, I would never do so.

Carefully I did not speak of my wish to Father. But I decided that I could use Philip. Uncle Doc was out. I could not use him. Philip would be the proper one. He knew of my frustrations over a medical career. He thought both my parents and I were wrong. Overriding their opposition, I should be studying medicine.

It was not difficult to use Philip. He was grateful if I would give him a date, he would have rather talked about other things on that date, but if I insisted . . .

Sure, I could observe. He thought I would do better to join a class observing surgery where there would be a lecture.

"You'll understand more, Joey," he ex-

plained. "And with a crowd of students —
most of 'em will wear white coats . . ."

"Can you get me one?"

"Oh, sure. And some wear dark glasses —
because of the lights, they say . . ."

"When can I do this?"

"I'll watch the schedule. When there is a
Fivecoat demonstration, and I'm free . . ."

"I could go on my own, maybe," I suggested

"I'd like to see you through."

Philip really was a sweet fellow. I always
was ashamed of my treatment of him, of my
lack of enthusiasm. What got into girls? I
asked myself, even then.

My father was a busy surgeon, and of
course on the faculty of the medical school,
so it was only a few days later that Philip
called me and told me to be ready, to take
two hours off at ten the next morning. "He's
doing a phrenic nerve."

"What's that?" I asked.

"You'll find out during the lecture, dum-
dum."

I laughed. "I never claimed not to be a
dum-dum," I told him.

"Can you get off?"

"Where will I meet you?"

He told me, and the next morning I did
meet him. He had brought the white jacket,

and I prided myself that I looked like one of the other medical students when we went into the amphitheater and found seats at the far end of the middle tier. There were at least twenty other young people ready to lean forward and observe the surgery to be performed.

Philip gave me a notebook like the one he carried. "Pretend to make notes," he said.

"Shhhh."

"We can hear the lecturer. Our voices don't go to the floor. Footscraping, coughs, and all that."

"Well, hush anyway, unless something needs to be explained."

He looked at me. "Joey?" he asked, his tone anxious.

"Yes. What is it?"

"You've never watched surgery before, have you?"

"No . . . course not."

"You won't — well, faint, or anything, at the sight of blood?"

"Don't be silly."

But, once he'd mentioned it, I wasn't sure, either, that I wouldn't.

Then of course I became so interested in the things going on . . . Philip kept up a running account of the case. "Hiccups are no joke," he told me. "This patient has been hiccuping for two months. She's not been able to eat, and her weight has gone way down . . ."

I watched the cart come in, I watched the swiftness and ease with which the patient was transferred to the table. There were nurses, other doctors — the resident, Philip told me. There were draped green sheets and folded green towels, and a shield between the patient's body and the anesthetist.

And that poor patient. Rhythmically, sixty times a minute — "Every second," said Philip, his tone awed — the women's whole body would be convulsed. I felt the spasm in my own body, and suffered along with the patient.

". . . brought her here from Louisiana," said Philip. "Dr. Fivecoat did this surgery three years ago. It was successful."

"Hush," I said to him again, for there, one of three gowned and masked men, was my father. Even as swathed and covered as he was, I would have known him anywhere. A sweep of his blond hair showed beneath his cap. There were his very blue eyes behind his round, sparkling eyeglasses. He was tall, and carried himself in a certain way. His hands — once he had dropped the towel, and showed his hands, in thin yellow rubber gloves —

And of course there was his voice . . .

I leaned forward, and Philip pulled me back. By then the benches were full. Several doctors were watching, as well as more students and some nurses. "Make notes," Philip whispered to me.

I realized only then that perhaps he had run some risk in bringing me to the demonstration; perhaps he had no business being there himself . . .

No one could ever have made sense of my "notes," because I never once let my gaze move from my father and what he was doing.

He talked a little about what he was going to do. The woman had lost weight until she was down to eighty-two pounds. He said she was, literally, starved. "Desperate measures are called for," said my father. He extended his gloved hand, and an instrument was slapped into it, hard.

"We shall cut into the neck — above the collarbone —" He did so, and there was the blood, though not much. Other hands sponged, held instruments —

"Retractors," said Philip.

". . . will expose the right phrenic nerve . . ."

I looked at the patient's eyes. She was under local anesthesia, and was still racked with those spasms of hiccups. She was watching

Father, much as I did, with hope, adoration, faith.

". . . and we will snip off an inch and a half of the nerve. Like a disconnected electric cord to a vibrator . . ." The hiccups slowed, stopped.

The patient said something, and the people close to the table laughed.

"She asked, 'When do I eat?' " said my father. His hands were still busy.

"The cutting," he explained, "stops the uncontrollable hiccups by disconnecting the diaphragm from the nervous impulses that caused the convulsions."

He stepped away from the table, carefully watching another doctor who was "closing up." I knew, without Philip's whisper, what was being done.

"Nerve cutting is a drastic operation," said my father. "We doctors know that we cannot predict all its effects. Like the vagus nerve operation for ulcers, and the prefrontal lobotomy for insanity, cutting the phrenic nerve impairs some internal functions, but doctors have observed no serious effects. My conclusion, like that of my colleagues, is that nerve cutting is justified as a last resort."

Well! I had seen my father operate. I left the amphitheater and the floor feeling both exhilarated and exhausted. Philip said I would need to learn to keep a hold on my emotions.

"I know," I agreed.

He was looking at me. "And you really do want to be a medic, don't you?" he asked.

"Oh, yes!" I breathed. "Oh, Philip, yes!"

"If you'd marry me, I'd let you."

I stared at him. "You're not serious!"

"Well, of course I'm serious. You know I've been fond of you ever since I was ten years old."

I patted his arm. "I'm fond of you, too," I told him. "But fond isn't enough."

I gave him his white jacket, and slipped into the elevator. It was only later that it occurred to me that he was serious, and I could have hurt him. I didn't want to do that. I *was* fond of Philip, but, oh, me, oh, my, I wasn't about to marry him!

I would find some other way to enter medical school. And as it happened, I did.

But just then — Of course I could not tell anyone about my o.r. experience. I could talk to Philip about it, and I would, but I probably would not see him for a day or so. I went back to the library, and home that evening, fizzing like a shaken bottle of soda. I considered telling Alice Peck what I had done. She would understand my rebellion, but she would not be interested in the ad-

venture itself. Medicine had no appeal whatever to her. She could not share my excitement about that!

So I kept still. I was not found out, and
this led me to think that I could do other
things. Small things, of course. Things like
asking to be transferred from the library duties to messenger service through the hospitals.

Now, communication is instant in any
large medical center, but at that time volunteers were used to carry all sorts of things
from the "floors" to the laboratories, X-rays
up to some doctor, records from the records
room . . .

We young people learned, often the hard
way, to value the trust put in us. It was
important that Dr. Winter have the X-rays
immediately! That blood and urine samples
get to the lab quickly and be carefully handled.

We did our work well, or we were out of
a job, and we had pride in it. I liked the
chance to know so many people, to understand some of the work they did.

And this led to the time — not in itself
important; I can see that now — when I
found myself brave enough to make a protest
to my parents, to argue with them.

Even my father and mother would have

laughed if they had known that bravery was required. They would have said that they were always open to a discussion of any point. They would have said that, and laughed gently at my foolishness.

But I found that some bravery was required, some courage.

The occasion was a charity carnival to be held on the parking lot of the big city's General Hospital.

Games would be played, balloons sold, food consumed, all to raise money for the mobile clinics which did so much good for the underprivileged of the city.

My father had, a time or two, taken us as children to similar charitable affairs, not really enjoying them himself. He always mentioned the noise and the confusion and the indigestible food. But we did go to such things. Occasionally.

So I decided at once that I could work at this carnival, and maybe my family would share by attending and supporting a worthwhile project which took a heavy load from all the health services in the city. The other hospitals gladly lent their support. Our big university-affiliated medical center did. Bulletins went up in every unit, and personnel were asked to volunteer to work at the carnival. I could tell that helping was the thing to do among the younger people. The names of volunteers quickly appeared on the bulletins. I wanted to add my own. Of course I would tell my parents what I planned but I could see no reason for any objection.

The cause was good. And though the neighborhood was admittedly a rough one, our medical center was going to provide a bus to transfer our workers downtown; there also would be controlled parking facilities. Aides, nurses, interns — all sorts of Center people were offering to help.

These volunteers would be asked to abide by certain rules and restrictions. The "young ladies" would be asked not to expose themselves to unfortunate "incidents." All workers would need to check in and out, just as they did for duty at the hospital.

It certainly sounded respectable. Talk about the affair, the feature articles in the newspapers, made it sound like fun. The city was urged to support the worthwhile project.

And I wanted to participate. There would be no danger. Other doctors were going to take their families to patronize the carnival. Surely my own family would attend. And watch me working at one of the booths.

I would ask them!

Chapter 4

Excitement about the carnival was encouraged throughout our complex. Books of tickets were on sale. I immediately bought two of these. I kept an eye on the posters put up on the various bulletin boards so workers could sign up, their duties and hours to be specified. Interns, nurses, aides, all scribbled their names on these posters and I longed to add mine. I would do anything!

Of course I would go! As the days went by, I became certain that the whole family would attend. This project was not only professionally endorsed, it was a charitable undertaking popular with the city's social and business leaders. I certainly should do my bit.

But because I still felt bound to get my parents' approval, I must secure their permission. I approached this problem first by asking if the family planned to attend the carnival. "It sounds like such fun," I said, "and the cause certainly is worthy."

"Joey wants a red balloon," Tread teased me.

I ignored him. My eyes were on Father.

He glanced at Tread, and at me. "I believe it is next week?" he said slowly.

"Yes. On the tenth. That afternoon and evening."

"The Pernoud dinner conflicts, I think," said Mother softly.

Father nodded and smiled at me. "I'll send a check, Joey," he told me. "A lot of the staff doctors are going to do that."

"Yes, I know, but couldn't I . . . ? I hoped maybe I could work at the carnival," I blurted.

"Oh, my dear," he protested.

"It's in a dreadfully grubby neighborhood, Joey," said Mother.

"Yes, but the Center is going to provide a bus for its workers. We'd be perfectly safe!"

"I — we've never been ones to mingle, my darling," said Father.

"But some of the Center doctors . . ."

"Not even to mingle with all of my professional colleagues," Father continued, as if I had not spoken. "Not in a social way, that is. We are getting all sorts, you know. All colors, and all nationalities. We doctors cannot possibly inflict some of these people on our families."

I stared at him, and at my mother. *Snobbery!* That was their trouble, and I wanted to throw their words back at them. Let them hear how they sounded! "Grubby neighborhood!" "All sorts, all colors, all nationalities . . ."

I swallowed all the things I could have shouted at my mother and father. By then I *knew* that I must work at the carnival. I must! "What about Uncle Doc?" I asked, breathlessly. "Isn't he going?"

"I really don't know," said Father, his tone indicating that the subject was closed.

In itself, the carnival was not all that important, but my parents' refusal to let me participate brought back all the pain and rebellion which I had felt, and suppressed nine months before when I was denied the right, the privilege, to study medicine. This time — I could submit. This time, I wanted — I *wanted* — to do things my way. At least, to try . . . I wanted to go to the carnival! I told Alice that I would ask Uncle Doc, but she said he would tell me that I was old enough to go on my own, or even to work at the carnival as other Volunteers were doing.

"I could work in the afternoon," I agreed.

"Sure you could. If it weren't for the hockey game, I'd go with you."

"You have to play, I know that. But,

Alice P! I am going to sign up!"

"You do that," she said, not realizing what a declaration I had just made.

And I did do it. The very next day at the hospital I signed my name. Joey Fivecoat. V for Volunteer. I would work at a booth. And I did not specify a time. I should have. I could have served from three until six, and probably no one at home would have needed to know that I was doing it.

But I was inexperienced at such things. Alice Peck would have known how, and would have done that. Within days the assignments were made. I was to work in the ice cream booth from six to nine.

I stared at the slip of paper giving me the time and place. I stared at my name when the schedules went up on the boards. Perhaps Father would see them and say something . . .

Uncle Doc knew about it. He said he thought it was fine for me to work at the carnival. "Take a footstool along, Joey," he told me. "So you can be seen over the counter."

He had always teased me about my size. I laid my armful of reports on his desk. "Are you going to the carnival?" I asked.

"If I don't have to work. Save a chocolate ice cream cone for me."

"I'll do that," I said, but I was shaking. I would have to tell my parents, and I had hoped I would say that Uncle Doc would be there.

The carnival was only three days away. That night at dinner I would have to say something. I so *wanted* to work, to be with the other hospital workers — people I knew and had come to like. I *had* to do it!

And there I was at the dinner table three evenings before the great day and I heard my mother asking my father something about the wine for the dinner. "Lillian has become rather tiresome about domestic wines," she said plaintively.

Lillian was Mrs. Pernoud, one of my mother's close friends.

Father was answering her. "You're the hostess, my dear," he reminded her.

I looked from one to the other. "I thought the Pernouds were giving the dinner," I blurted.

"No, dear, we are. I'll need you . . ."

I almost rose from my chair. "But I can't!" I cried excitedly. "That's the night of the General Hospital carnival! I am going to be working at the ice cream booth!"

I caught my father's tolerant smile.

"Oh, no, darling," said Mother softly. Firmly.

I shall never forget that dinner table. We were using the blue and white Haviland service. The damask tablecloth's pattern was of chrysanthemums, and there was a low, silver bowl of pink roses for a centerpiece. Mother was wearing a dull green dress, with a white pin — jade, perhaps — among the ruffles at her throat.

I sat there staring at my mother. Leaning toward her. "But why not?" I cried, my voice harsh.

Mother looked to Father to answer me, and he did. He touched his napkin to his lips and his small mustache. "Because of one important reason, Joey dear," he said quietly. "Your name is Fivecoat."

So my name was Fivecoat. Joey Fivecoat. I could feel my cheeks getting red. And hot.

"I run errands all over the hospital," I cried. "Everyone knows I am your daughter."

"That is true. May I point out that, in the hospital, you are protected. While at the carnival . . ."

I could see what was threatening, and wildly I fought back.

"But who needs protecting?" I cried. "If I go with the hospital group. . . . What difference should it make to them? My being your daughter?"

My father answered me gently. Lovingly. "Doesn't it make a difference, Joey?" he asked.

I could feel tears crowding into my eyes. I gulped them back. "Not to me on this occasion!" I cried. "And it makes no difference to the people at the Center. No one seems to notice who I am."

My father nodded. "The key word of that statement," he said, still tolerantly, "would be the word *seems,* my darling." He picked up his fork to resume eating his dinner.

I was bitterly disappointed. I could feel life going on about me — exciting, interesting life. But it was all passing me by. I was not sharing it; maybe I never would share it.

I didn't talk to Alice Peck, or to anyone, about my disappointment. But she knew how I felt, and she went to Mother.

"I don't believe you realize how deeply disappointed Joey is, Mother, in not being allowed to work at the General Hospital carnival."

"Oh, Alice, darling, I am sorry. What has she said?"

"Nothing. She won't say anything. But this is something she did want to do."

"Yes, I suppose she did."

"Any other girl would go anyway."

Mother sat thoughtful. "Of course she has no idea of what it would be like."

"Why not let her find out? She can't be sheltered forever, kept in a box, Mother. It won't work. If you and Father continue to frustrate her . . . She's old enough now — We don't want her to do anything foolish, of course. She's such a dear one . . ."

They were in the library; I had come along the hall, heard their voices, and stopped, frankly listening.

"Do you think we do frustrate her, Alice Peck?" Mother's voice was a small one, but it rang clearly, and sweetly.

"Oh, sure you do!" came Alice Peck's much more vigorous tones. "You really, really do, Mother! You do keep her in that box I mentioned."

"I don't believe I understand you on that point, dear. If you mean our home . . ."

"I mean," said Alice, "our life in this home. We . . ."

I prayed that no one would come into the hall so that I would have to move along to the stairs. Where I was, the hall was rather narrow, with doors opening from it. The half-open one into the library, the closed one of a coat closet, and another into the powder room. The walls were painted a creamy beige, the wood trim was white. There was a small Oriental rug where I was standing, and against the wall, between two of the doors, there was a small chest with a telephone on it, a slender vase with, that evening, a few daisies and three red tulips arranged in it. One of the scarlet flowers drooped heavily, beautifully. There was a small mirror above the table, and in it I could see myself. I wore my hair longer then, to my shoulders. It was soft and fine and fell in shallow waves about my face. My eyes were huge.

I was not thinking of how I looked, I was so intently listening to what Mother was saying to Alice Peck. I was grateful that my sister had the courage . . .

". . . we have such good times together, darling," Mother was saying. "The things we all do together — we have so much fun."

"Yes, we do. But Joey's grown up, Mother. When I am her age, I'll want to think about a life of my own."

"I know, dear. She and you both will marry . . ."

"And have beautiful weddings. Yes, we'll probably do that too. But Joey, at least, has ideas about a career. She did want to study medicine, you know. She really did!"

"Your dear father doesn't think it is a field for women."

"And so he frustrated our dear Joey!" I heard the sharp tone in my sister's voice. "He put her back into the box. He doesn't want to believe there is a world beyond that box. But there is, Mother, and Joey knows there is."

I moved on then. When Alice Peck came upstairs, I was in our room, pretending to read. I felt sure she knew, somehow, that I had overheard her and Mother. But she didn't say one word about it.

The next day was my half-day at the hospital, and at breakfast Mother asked me if I would like to go to the florist's with her and select flowers for her dinner party.

Of course I said I would go. I don't believe I sounded either grumpy or overly placid. I often went with Mother on such errands. She made all the decisions, but the short walk together through the city's sunny streets was pleasant.

That morning I was not going to be pleasant or unpleasant. I was feeling hollow, and don't-care-about-everything.

We started out, Mother, as always, wearing a hat and gloves. "Your hair will blow, darling," she said, by way of suggesting that I, too . . .

"It won't get too messy," I promised. "I'm thinking of cutting it short."

"Oh, Joey!" This sweetly protesting.

"Tread's hair has a lovely wave, and is coarse, easy to handle, Alice Peck has naturally curly hair. Why did I get this fine stuff anyway?"

"It's a beautiful color."

I nodded. We walked along. To the corner, across the street.

"Joey," said Mother. "Do you really want so much to work at that rowdy carnival?"

I stopped walking. "Yes!" I said emphatically. "I really would like to do it, Mother. And I don't think it is fair to call it rowdy. It won't be. Crowded and noisy, maybe, but mainly it will just be a lot of young people having fun."

"I see," said Mother.

I opened the door of the florist's shop. "In a good cause," I added.

That was all that was said. We — I — liked the florist's shop, the lovely, earthy smell of it. The cans and jars of new flowers sitting around that morning; there were dozens and dozens of carnations. Heaps of huckleberry and fern. A large wedding was being prepared for. . . .

Mother talked to the proprietor. I didn't really listen. I had discovered the pale yellow carnations, fresh, spicy, lovely. And as we left, the man gave me one, bowing and smiling. "It's the color of your hair, Miss Joey," he told me.

We walked home again, talking about the wedding. I put the carnation into a bud vase on my dressing table.

That afternoon, I worked at the hospital, and I did not take my name off the workers' list, nor say anything to anybody about not being able to work at the carnival. I still had two days, and something could happen.

It did. Mother decided to go to my father and talk to him. I knew — I know now — that this must have taken a great amount of courage on her part. My father, literally, adored my mother. I am sure that she never defied him, nor crossed him, that she very seldom questioned his judgment. If this was to be one of those times . . . I didn't know what she had in mind, or I would have told her that this would not be a good time to upset him further than he already was being upset over a speech Uncle Doc had made that same week.

I had heard him make parts of that speech in the library of our home as he argued the matter with Father. As I still occasionally could do, I was reading in a corner of the room while Uncle Doc and Father enjoyed their after-dinner brandy and talked shop.

"I am amazed that the Anti-vivisectionists are still at it," Uncle Doc told Father. "They certainly don't give up, do they? But here they are, wanting to address our Medical Society meeting."

"They want it to be an open meeting, Dick," said Father.

"Sure they do. Open to all the sob-sisters and do-gooders. Do-gooders to stray cats and dogs, not to children. Lordy me, Paul — You don't suppose they are hoping to get an election on that subject here in this city or state, do you?"

"What I don't see is why you should undertake to answer them."

"Experience, Paul. Experience. I began way back in forty-eight, talking to these nuts. That was in Los Angeles. They really take on movements out there, you know. At that time, these Tail-Waggers and Mercy Crusaders were tying up the adequate supply of animals for research in radiation. And they played pure hob with old Goldblatt when he was trying to develop a heart-lung machine. Way back then, Paul! Way back then." Uncle Doc paced the floor in his agitation.

"I know, Dick," said Father. "But why should you . . . ?"

"You think an orthopod should shut up and let you gut men do the talking."

"I don't think any of us should seek to publicize the matter."

"The Anti-vivs want the open meeting. That means reporters. Arid I plan to give the pencil pushers something to write about. Don't fear, the Anti-vivs will bring in their fake pictures of tortured dogs, and tell their grisly tales. They'll call the researchers everything from fiends to ghouls, to sadists and murderers.

"Why, I remember, Paul — we won the battle in L.A. and then we fought it again in Baltimore. In the city where Johns Hopkins and Helen Taussig, even by then, had saved thousands of blue babies through a technique developed after a long, long course of experiments on dogs.

"The dogs got care and anesthesia, just as the children did, just as both of 'em do now. And not all the dogs died, or the technique would have been called a failure."

Now Uncle Doc was sitting again in his deep leather chair, chuckling a little over his memories.

"You had to learn on dogs, Paul. You know you did. You didn't get your skill, on stomachs and intestines without learning how on dogs. We couldn't, we can't, afford monkeys, and except in the laboratories, mice and rats and guinea pigs won't do. We have to use dogs, because their tissues and organs closely resemble man's, not because we hate dogs. Rubinstein didn't learn to be the pianist he is without a keyboard. Hundreds and millions of men and women are alive today because we men learned to open the chest and abdomen by practicing on stray dogs. Where would insulin and penicillin be without our experiments? Maybe the Anti-vivs can tell us that."

"I just hate to have you bring that row all up again, Dick."

"Someone has to. And I'll do it. I'll pull out all the stops in my organ, too. I'll ask the old cliché. Do you care to choose a healthy, happy child, or a mongrel stray?"

"You wouldn't . . ."

"Damn right, I'll bring in the child, *and* the stray. And be sure the television camera is working! I don't know, these days, if the child will be hissed and the cur cheered, but I'll bet my last dime that somebody suggests we use mental patients, or prisoner bums from the jails for our practice rather than homeless, hungry dogs."

It must have been a grand speech. The hospital folk delighted in it; there had been full publicity. Uncle Doc beamed about it, and Father shook his head in despair.

So, while he was still in that mood, it was

not the best time for Mother to tell him that he — that *they* — perhaps could change their minds and allow me to go to the hospital carnival.

I was not present, of course. I can only imagine the scene as it probably happened. Father would have been surprised, I am sure, that Mother would speak up against some decision he had made.

He probably would have glanced up at her, then he would have frowned a little and laid his newspaper to one side. "What's that you say?" he could have asked.

Mother's cheeks would get a little pink, and her breath would come faster. Perhaps she would have fingered the pin she usually wore at the throat of her dress.

"Joey is such a good child," she would have pointed out.

"My goodness, I certainly hope so!"

"She is," said Mother. "And she does let us guide her about everything she does. But — this carnival — I am sure she remembers the times that we took the children to things like it when they were younger. Now that she is helping at the hospital, perhaps it is natural that she would want to do her part toward this worthwhile project. You could determine this, but I would be inclined to think that those in charge would not let anything unfortunate occur among the young people."

"Oh, yes, I suppose that is true. The Center would take steps to protect itself and its reputation."

"Of course. And the young people do need fun, Paul."

"Yes, yes. I just dislike to expose my girls to — well — distasteful things."

"We have been very conscientious in the way we have raised the children, Paul."

Perhaps Father thought that this self-evident statement needed no comment.

"Joey is an especially well-disciplined person, Paul. She can certainly judge for herself if the carnival presents any situation that her tastes will not enjoy. She has never given us any reason to think otherwise."

I can only guess what was said that evening. I know that my mother sought me out where I was — in the garden behind our house. The evening was a warm one, and I had decided to check on the tree house. I found that it had been dismantled and taken down, sometime during my last year at college, Alice Peck told me.

"We're supposed to be growing up," she said.

"Oh, go play your hockey game!" I retorted. But I was sorry about the tree house. I wasn't sure, just then, that I was ready to enjoy growing up.

Then Mother came down into the garden, softly calling my name.

We talked a little about the tree house and about the rosebushes. Then Mother told me what she and Father had decided. "You must be very careful, Joey," she cautioned me. "Your dear father consented only reluctantly."

I promised her that I would be very careful! I would have promised anything, *anything*! I was wildly ecstatic, and excited entirely out of proportion to the affair's importance.

The carnival would be the next night! I must be sure I had a starchy-clean pinafore. That my white shoes were clean. Maybe I should buy a new pair? I'd wash my hair that night . . .

Mother watched me, smiling slightly. I kissed her and thanked her. "Did you say you would need to be there between six and nine, dear?" she asked.

"Yes. On duty at the ice cream stand. I'll need to go a little earlier. Anyway, I would want to look at the other stands before and after my hours of duty."

"We could expect you home by ten?"

"I'll try. It would depend on the bus schedule."

I was prepared for her to say that she would have Hermann fetch me. But just at that minute, Alice called from our bedroom window that there was a phone call for me.

Mother followed me inside, softly assuring herself, and me, that Alice *knew* she should not *shout* from the window . . .

The caller was Philip Winter, and Mother, standing beside me in the hall, smiled and nodded when I said, "Oh, hello, Philip."

He told me that he had seen my name on the list of carnival workers. "I'll drive you down. I can manage that just fine . . ."

I told him there was no need. I planned to use the bus which the Center was providing.

Mother touched my arm. "Let him take you, Joey!" she whispered. "Your dear father and I will feel better about your going."

I sighed, and said all right to Philip. "Pick me up here about five," I told him. "And thank you, Philip." I hung up.

Mother was pleased, and already making plans.

"You don't want to eat the things they serve, dear. Before you go I'll have a light supper for you and Philip in the breakfast room. You know, with my dinner party . . ."

I stared at her. Had she, or Father, asked Philip . . . ? "Oh, Mother!"

"What's wrong, dear? He'll watch out for you, and you and Philip are such good friends."

Yes, we were. But why did someone, anyone, have to "watch out" for me? Why couldn't I have ridden the bus and been on my own?

I didn't quite say it to Mother, but I felt that I would just as soon give up the carnival. If I couldn't go with a group of young people, have fun, and come home again . . . I did not need *watching!*

I did say that much to Mother, and she only smiled and said, "We are going to feel better, Joey."

"I just won't go at all!" I stormed to Alice Peck when I went up to our room and told her what had happened.

She had been studying, and she listened to all I had to say. "You'd better calm down, Joey," she told me quietly.

"But, *Alice!*"

"Look. You wanted to go to the carnival. You were pretty desperate about wanting to go. Weren't you?"

"Yes, I was, but —"

"Well, you are going. If it seems that you are not getting everything you wanted, the way you wanted it . . . What difference does it make if Philip drives you downtown, and then brings you home again?"

"And watches out for me while I am there!" I threw myself on the bed.

"He won't. He will have his own fun while you are dipping ice cream. By the way, do you know how to use an ice cream scoop?"

I never had used one. And I laughed a little. "I'm sorry, Alice P."

"Okay. I wish I could go and watch you myself. D'you have a clean uniform?"

"I was going to check. And on my shoes . . ." I got off the bed.

"And you'll let me study, I hope," said Alice. "I've been taking trigonometry this year. Did you know that?"

"Why?"

"To get myself educated, that's why."

"All that, and hockey, too," I teased, rumpling her hair as I passed her.

"Yeah, hockey. We have that game tomorrow, and a banquet after it. I don't know which needs more practice for."

"I'll lend you Philip to help get you through."

She turned away from the desk. "Look," she said. "Don't be so damn hard on Philip."

"And don't you say *damn*."

She nodded. "I shouldn't, should I? But,

111

Joey, really — Philip's a good-looking guy. No! Strike that. I shouldn't say *guy* either. But he is good-looking, and you'll have other girls who will envy you for the way he hangs around. You couldn't keep him from going to the carnival on his own; he's a med student and probably will help out the same as you will. Besides, he does like you, Joey. He always has. I mean, he's going to be *glad* to watch out for you."

I nodded. "I know," I agreed. "I should be nicer to him. And I shall be tomorrow, if only because I am so glad to go to the carnival."

And we did go. We had our supper served in the breakfast room — chicken in patty shells, I think. And we departed, wondering where Philip would park his car. If the hospital parking lot was being used for the carnival . . . "We'll have to walk blocks!" said Philip. We did.

I was proud to wear my pink pinafore on the street. It marked me as a helper at the carnival, and the name tag read simply "Joey." There was no Fivecoat name to be recognized and sullied.

Chapter 5

Almost everything one remembers from childhood diminishes in size when viewed as an adult. That was not true of the carnival. Probably because we children had been limited to a very small part of the grounds of such carnivals as we attended, and saw very little of the over-all fun and games.

Going there that evening, hearing the music as we approached, seeing the crowds of people — that was all familiar, as were the balloons and the smell of popcorn. But I was not prepared for the size of the undertaking. Nor the *bigness* of the crowds.

"This is good," Philip decided at once. And he explained to me that General Hospital's parking lot covered a whole city block.

"I had never realized," I confessed, "that it would be so large!"

"Are you frightened?"

I looked up at him. "Of course not!" I told him indignantly. "I'm just surprised. . . ."

He reminded me that we were supposed to check in. As we made our way to this place, he told me that he had worked for a couple of hours early in the afternoon.

"What did you do?"

"I blew up balloons. And don't tell me that I'm the one who could do it. I had a machine."

I giggled and let him hold my arm so we wouldn't get separated. The carnival, I decided, was noisy, it was fun, but I wouldn't have called it rowdy. The booths were set up in two rows, red and white pennants blew in the breeze. Uniformed candy-stripers, aides, Volunteers, nurses, students and interns worked at the booths. Everyone called everyone else by his or her first name, regardless of age or hospital affiliation.

It appeared that too many had signed up for the ice cream booth, or, at least, had been assigned to it. I was asked if I'd mind working somewhere else. Of course I said I didn't mind before finding out what the other booth was, and Philip teased me — with help from others — about being the victim at the plunge, where someone was dunked into a huge tub of water if the player could throw a baseball accurately enough.

I refused to be frightened or teased. I knew he wouldn't have exposed me to that. He was afraid of my father.

"Just tell me where the right booth is," I

said confidently, "and I'll do it."

"She needs a bath anyway," Philip assured those in on his joke.

I jingled the money I had put in my pockets. "We have a few minutes," I told Philip. "I want to buy a balloon and some popcorn and some souvenirs . . ."

"And I'll have to carry them while you work."

"Of course. You wouldn't want such things to get wet, would you? I'm going to buy a pink plush poodle, too."

He groaned. "Okay, okay."

We made the most of our time, and had fun. We even rode the carousel which had been set up for children. We slid down the slides into a pile of foam rubber. We bought a red balloon and ate popcorn, and talked to a dozen people I didn't know. They were the workers from other hospitals. Charitably minded residents from all over the city patronized the carnival. A lot of doctors brought their families. I don't think I had ever known so many openly friendly people gathered in one place.

We met Uncle Doc, who asked me where I was working. I looked at Philip.

"At the white elephant booth." Philip would not dare to suggest that I would be even close to a coconut shy.

Even so, Uncle Doc said he would not come near me.

"All right," I told him. "I'll give you my plush poodle. You can't leave here without something useless!"

We hurried away before he could refuse the animal I thrust into his arms. I suppose he gave it to some child. I never saw the thing again. It was most terribly pink.

But I enjoyed working in my booth, where I must try to sell what I called "useless articles." "Nobody wants them, but we have to sell them," I would coax anyone who came near.

Philip hung around for a while and helped, too, then he wandered off. I was having a wonderful time. I had always thought myself shy, but there must have been a peddler in my ancestry, because I found I could call out to passers-by, I could do a hard sell on a really hideous vase, or a sofa cushion no one could possibly want.

I found that my phrase — *the booth of useless articles* — was being used and repeated. Our booth became a popular place, and we just about sold out on everything we had. I was very pleased at what I considered my success.

And I had more fun than I could remember ever having before. The loud-speakers

116

boomed, Elvis Presley records were played loudly and persistently. There was an eager young man who kept hanging around.

"You have to buy something if you keep leaning on our counter," I told him.

So he bought a box of really awful fruit knives, and the older woman, a nurse from St. Luke's who worked with me, told me to have a little pity. "He couldn't possibly want those knives, Joey."

"We're here to sell the dumb things. If he doesn't want to buy something, he can go elsewhere."

"He wants to ask you for a date," said the nurse. Her name was Hannah.

"Who is he?" I asked, straightening some embroidered tea towels. "Do you know?"

"Oh, yes. His name is Gary. That's on his tag. But he works in X-ray at University. He's a technologist, I think. And he really has fallen for you."

"It's a gag," I assured her.

"Well, his extravagance may be — but — well, be kind to the boy, Joey."

"I doubt if he'll get his date."

But, as any girl would be, I was pleased at the attention this crazy technologist, or whatever, was paying me. He hung around, he said silly things — and finally he did mention taking me somewhere after the carnival.

"I have to sweep up," I told him.

"I'll help you. I'll hold your dustpan. I'll kneel at your feet and hold the pan . . ."

I laughed at him. I wouldn't have any trouble avoiding a date with him, but I was reassured by the fact that Philip seemed to be close by most of the time. He and a group of young people from the Center — I knew some of them, medical students, a clerk from Admissions, another Volunteer — were waiting for me to be through my assigned hours.

Hannah, the nurse, told me I could leave early if I wanted. "We seem to be sold out, dear," she told me.

"Should I go back and be assigned somewhere else?"

There was still twenty minutes.

"No, you go on. Eat hot dogs, and dance. I'll close this operation down. If you go now, you may escape Gary. Provided you want to escape him."

I did. I said good night to Hannah, gave the cash box to the guard who came around regularly to take care of such things, and I ducked under the counter, ready to run down to where Philip was waiting.

When I stood erect, someone seized my arm. I think I may have screamed a little — because I was startled, not hurt. Philip came running, shouting, and several people

118

turned. Hannah leaned over the counter. "Are you all right, Joey?" she asked.

"I'm fine," I said, pulling away from Gary. "What are you trying to *do?*" I asked him.

"That's a fair question," said Philip angrily.

"Hey, lay off!" cried Gary. "I was just waiting for my date."

The incident was more embarrassing than anything else. I had not really made any date with Gary; Philip was going to drive me home. "If that's your idea of a date," I said to Gary, disgusted because of the small crowd which had been attracted by the fracas, "it won't take a thing to break it."

Someone of our group suggested that we get out of there — go have something to eat — and we started off, leaving Gary standing there alone, looking baffled.

So of course Philip felt sorry for him; after all, this was a hospital project — if the fellow worked at the Center . . .

"Come along," he invited. "We're going to get something to eat."

Philip really was a nice guy, as Alice Peck had said. Now I wish he had not been. But that evening, all of us were friends together, and the small flurry before our booth was quickly forgotten.

A few tables had been set up at one corner

of the big parking lot. Here one could order sandwiches, milk shakes, ice cream — things like that.

I found that I was hungry, and the ham and lettuce sandwich tasted wonderfully good. I sat between Philip and the Admissions clerk, with the Gary-character — his last name was Clark — beyond her. We talked about the carnival, and told funny things that had happened, and I don't recall just how the talk turned on ways in which we could evade the restrictions placed upon us and escape the "Dragons."

"What dragons?" I asked Philip.

"Oh, the chaperons."

I stared at him. "I didn't know we had any."

"Shhh. Your innocence is showing. They are those older people — volunteers — that nurse who worked in your stand — men and women stationed where they can supervise things and keep the party from getting rowdy. They don't want this bonanza carnival to earn a bad name. Remember? You dames are not supposed to expose yourselves to incidents."

We all laughed at that.

"That's why we have to check in and check out," the Admissions clerk explained to me.

"Aren't they being extra fussy?" I asked.

"I don't believe other hospital groups are so closely supervised."

"I asked about that, and the answer I got was that they were reminded that they were adults . . ."

"And we're not?"

"Well, maybe the Center doesn't want us to prove that we are. Or not."

Later I really was to appreciate the Center's precautions, but that night I could laugh with the others when Gary Clark called them vigilantes. "I bet I could escape them," he boasted.

The block-big parking lot was enclosed by a ten-foot steel wire fence, the windowed, high walls of City General forming the fourth side. Ticket booths and turnstiles, the check-in desk, stretched across the wide driveway into the street. I had noticed uniformed guards stationed there and patroling the street outside the fence. To keep people out, not to keep us in.

Someone was telling Gary that he could just take off his nameplate and walk down the driveway, out of the grounds. He was wearing a white shirt and dark trousers. He might have been one of the patrons of the carnival.

"I don't think he looks rich enough," said one of the girls, and we all laughed.

"But you could leave that way," Philip agreed.

"I couldn't take Joey with me, in her pink apron."

"You couldn't take Joey, period," I assured him, and the others laughed again. They were in the mood to laugh at anything.

One of the couples got up to dance on the blacktop, and when Gary Clark asked me I couldn't refuse without being really rude. Besides, I loved to dance.

He was an exceptionally good dancer, and I enjoyed myself. When we came back to the table, Philip said he and I should be leaving.

"She's Cinderella," he explained to the others, and his saying that irritated me. It brought to mind all the restrictions I knew at home, and which he knew about, too, in contrast to the freedom and fun I'd had that evening.

"I hate to leave," I said.

"Well, in another hour, it will be everybody out!" said Gary. "Before that, who'll bet me that I can't get Joey out without checking?"

Nobody seemed to want to bet. Someone did say that he wouldn't do it and get himself in trouble. And me.

"Heck!" Gary cried. "I wouldn't get her

into *trouble!* And I do mean to do it." His eyes were bright. He stood up and held his hand out to me.

Everyone spoke at once. Some said he couldn't! Some said, "Go on, Joey! Do it!" I was considerably flustered. Afterward, I tried to figure what was happening to me. I didn't like Gary Clark very much, but I was excited — the whole evening, the freedom and the fun. The dancing I'd done . . . Of course I was tired, too, though I didn't know that, then. And there was Philip, acting bossy; he kept saying he wouldn't allow it! Yes, he did have a right; he was my cousin.

"That's ridiculous!" I said.

Gary Clark was standing behind my chair, still holding out his hand to me. "Why pick on me?" I asked him. I was half afraid to defy Philip and do whatever Gary had in mind.

"It would be fun," said someone. And it would be.

"There can't much of anything happen," said someone else.

"Aw, he'll just walk down the drive with her," said one of the med students.

"No, I won't," Gary insisted. "We'll do a proper escape, through the ambulance garage, up the stairs — the whole bit."

I laughed at that, and I looked up at Philip.

123

"Not much of anything can happen," I told him.

"Maybe not," he agreed, "but Doctor and Mrs. Fivecoat gave me charge of you tonight, and —"

That was what I had thought! "I'm going!" I said, defying his anger.

I remember the excitement. The others were to stay at the table, not follow or give us away. I still can feel the tingle of holding Gary's hand, going between the booths, among the people, clear to the bulk of the hospital itself. I had never known such a thrill. At college, other girls had broken rules, never me . . .

We found the ambulance entrance blocked. So — what would we do? Go back? Check out at the desk? I had an escort and could properly leave.

But that was too tame for Gary, though what he did was simple enough.

Two doors into the hospital basement had been kept open for the convenience of the carnival workers. Gary led me through the one marked MEN, holding my hand tight against my protest.

We ran past the employees' locker rooms and toilets, opened a door marked STAIRS, ran up them, then came out into the hospital's first floor corridor — where we certainly

124

had no business to be! We walked swiftly through this tunnel of bright ceiling lights, green walls, waxed floors, doors and doors, past a white-coated orderly and a Gurney cart, finally reaching a glass-windowed swinging door, and through it out to the front vestibule and steps of the big hospital.

Gary said he had a car parked a block away. "Run, Joey . . ."

I didn't want to run. "We can go back now," I gasped.

He laughed. "We'll drive around the block first."

And probably honk the horn at our friends inside the fence. I would have refused. I should have refused, but too often — a time or two — I had heard myself called priggish. I got into the car.

"We'll get a Coke," said Gary, starting the thing. It was old and noisy; it bounced and rattled down the street.

"They have Cokes at the carnival," I reminded him.

He looked at me, laughing. "But they're legal, Joey!" he cried. "They're *legal!*"

I decided then that he was not going to take me back to the carnival, and he did not. We drove straight across the city on the Freeway, turned off on the Boulevard, and from there into the park. I no longer felt like laughing. I wished I were back at the carnival, letting old sober and dependable Philip take me home . . .

In those days the park was not as dangerous as it is now. Then — the lagoons gleamed darkly, the bridges arched like paler shadows. We passed a couple of other cars, parked. We — Gary — parked his. I planned desperately. We were half a mile from my house. If I could give this Gary-character the slip, I could walk home.

Even as I planned, I sat where I was, shivering, though it was a warm spring night. Gary came around and held out his hand to me.

"I think you'd better take me home," I said faintly.

But he seized my hand and pulled me out of the seat. Still holding my hand, he drew me into his arms. I stiffened and tried to pull free, and he held me tightly, roughly.

When he tried to kiss me, I fought him, turning my head away; then he got really rough.

He said something about my being entirely too cold. "Forget your name is Fivecoat," he said. "Remember you're just a girl!" He had his head down against my shoulder, and he was kissing — almost biting — my throat. He was strong, and hot. His shirt was wet.

"Forget I'm a lab worker, too!" he said gruffly.

I fought him, and he wrestled with me. He used his leg and knee to hold my legs against the bridge railing; he used his body to press me back, and back . . .

Once I did manage to break free, and I ran, but he caught me, seizing my arm, pulling me toward him so roughly that I felt my neck snap. I was crying, begging in terror. . . .

He grabbed the bib of my pinafore, and I felt the stitches give —

"Hold it!"

I have never heard so beautiful a voice in my life. I could never hear anything so wonderful, so welcome . . .

It stopped Gary short enough that again I slipped free. Philip only glanced at me. "My car is at the far end of the bridge, Joey," he said, sounding very grown-up and strong. "You wait there for me."

Of course I ran. I stumbled once and skinned my knee on the roadway. I was sobbing when I found Philip's little car and scrambled into it. I pushed my hair out of my eyes, and felt of my clothes. That devil had torn my pinafore, and my blouse was up out of it. My skinned knee hurt. I wanted to go home. My parents . . .

I looked back along the bridge to see if

Philip was coming. But he and that Gary were fighting. Under the lights on the bridge I could see their arms flailing. I saw Gary grab Philip as he had grabbed me — and I saw . . . I saw Philip go flying over the bridge railing, his legs and arms grotesque against the lamplight. . . .

I got out of his car and ran back along the bridge, looked over the cement railing — and down there, in the shadows, Philip was lying, half in the water.

I was crying again, and I looked along the shadowy lagoon. Could I get down the slope to him? I knew he was hurt. He lay so still.

Gary Clark knew it, too. He joined me on what looked to be the lowest part of the sloping bank. I slipped and slid, refusing to let him help me.

"I've blown it for sure," he said, and then repeated himself.

I finally reached Philip. And, just looking at him, I knew that he was dead. I waded into the water and lifted his head against my breast. There was an awful cut, and blood on his forehead where he had struck the sharp rock.

I stood there in the scummy water, and I knew just exactly how terrible things were going to be. And it was my fault. My fault.

Chapter 6

And things began to be terrible right away. Gary Clark panicked, and I did, each behaving, I suppose, in his own way, in the way his background had conditioned him.

"The dumb cluck had to follow us!" cried Gary angrily. "All the way . . ."

I heard what he said, but my mind was full of other things. Everything swirled through my mind at once. The way Gary Clark had tricked me — and threatened me . . .

My father had not wanted me to go to the carnival . . . And he had been right!

And Philip . . . Oh, poor, *poor* Philip!

I knelt beside him and wept.

"I — I'm sorry about your cousin," said Gary.

I shook the tears from my face. "He's not my cousin!" I sobbed.

"It was an accident . . ." said Gary.

I stood up and faced him. "You were fighting!"

"Yes. We were. But he lost his balance — and went over the rail."

I had seen him go over, his long legs pinwheeling, his arms and hands reaching, clutching —

I wept bitterly. And Gary tried to comfort me. I would not let him touch me. I *loathed* him!

"What are we going to do?" he asked me.

"I want to go home!"

He shook his head. "Look at you! You're wet to your waist. Blood and muck all over you. . . ."

"I don't care. I want to go home!"

"Yeah. And old Fivecoat would kill you and me both."

"You killed Philip!"

"I did not. I tell you, he fell."

I kept sobbing, and I turned away from him to climb up the bank again. If I could clean up a little . . .

"Maybe we should go back to the carnival," I said, "and not say anything about this."

He laughed. He really did. But it was a bitter laugh. "I suppose you got to looking the way you do because we went through the men's locker room."

"Well, what *are* we going to do?" I demanded.

He was as frightened as I was, and as angry, too. "We'll have to get help . . ." he said gruffly.

I stared at him. All about us were the park lights, the circles of brightness, the dark shadows in between. We heard a car go along the road and across the bridge above us — and we waited breathlessly. But it went on, and then the park was quiet again.

"If you mean the police," I whispered, "they're not going to believe that you didn't kill Philip, that he fell . . ."

"We, sweetheart. *We*," Gary amended.

I nodded. "They will have to know . . ."

"They sure will," he agreed. "And when they come, you can tell them how I tried to rape you —"

That was when I came close to fainting. I went icy-cold, and my arms tingled.

Gary did not notice. We were climbing up the bank. "Your cousin came after us and saved you, defended your virtue . . ." he was continuing; I saw that he was getting angrier and more scared by the minute.

He turned. "I didn't do one damn thing," he shouted at me, "but try to kiss you!"

I suppose I sniffed, or something. It is hard to imagine such a scene. With a dead man lying there on the bank below us, we talked about . . .

"Haven't you ever been kissed before?" Gary demanded, his tone still angry. "It can be fun, you know. It could have been tonight. Besides, you should know how to defend your own virtue, and not drag a good guy like Winter into it."

And there I was, weeping again. "I suppose — you're saying I'm to blame?"

"Like I said, Joey, we're in this together. You're to blame as much as anyone."

That time I couldn't stop weeping. "Please do something," I begged. "I have to get home!"

Though what would happen when I did get there could not be thought about.

"Can you drive?" Gary asked me.

"Ye-es." But I didn't want to drive. Not his old car, and certainly not Philip's.

He saw that I couldn't be asked to drive. He said for me to wait while he . . .

But I certainly did not want to stay there alone on that bridge! So he said we'd go together. If we didn't meet a policeman, their headquarters were close by . . .

And right away we did find a mounted policeman. We told him about Philip's fall.

I can remember sitting there and thinking, of all things, about the way Alice Peck loved horses. I feared them; this one's big eyes were to haunt my dreams for weeks to come. But Alice Peck . . .

I don't suppose we were coherent, but the policeman seemed to piece out our story. Of course we had to go back to the bridge, and we watched the tall, booted man slip and slither down the bank to Philip.

The horse waited, stomping a foot now and then. And the policeman came up again and used a sort of walkie-talkie thing to ask for an ambulance. He told us to go sit in the car — and not talk to anyone. By then a couple of other cars had come along. I didn't want to sit with Gary, but I did, hunched forward and shivering.

The ambulance driver recognized my name and said I should ride to the hospital — my father could fetch me from there. I suppose this saved me from going to the police station, though a half dozen people did question me. It was all a confusion of men bending over me, one of them a doctor whom I had last seen at the carnival, and finally my father came, looking white, but very clean and precisely dressed. He held me close, and wouldn't let me talk.

He kept things that way. And I was grateful for our sheltered home. I knew the reporters kept the phone busy, the police came, my mother went about like a ghost — she blamed herself for saying I should go to the carnival — even Alice didn't talk about what had happened.

"Did Father tell you not to?" I asked her.

133

"Ye-es. But he is right, Joey. You must forget this —"

I shook my head. "I never will," I told her.

Those hours — those next days — soon became like one of those glass balls we used to have at Christmas-time. There would be a picture, a scene of a child on a sled, or of a Christmas tree, then if the ball were tipped, one saw only swirling "snow." After a time the picture would reappear. Time became like that for me, and it still seems that things happened, with no sequence or meaning . . .

Eventually Alice did talk to me about the awful night. In the privacy of our room . . . "I hope she can sleep," I had heard Mother whisper at the door.

Alice made me take a warm bath, and she bundled me into a warm, fleecy robe — it was pink — and she turned down my bed.

Then she sat beside me and held my hand. "Maybe if you talked about it . . ." she faltered. At the time I forgot how strange all this must be for Alice Peck, too. She was just barely seventeen, and her experience was at least as small as my own. But that night I leaned upon her, and after a time I did talk.

I think it helped. And I did need any help I could find. The whole event — I was both inside and out of that ball of swirling, blinding events. There was the inquest. Father, and everyone, tried to keep me from that. But the authorities were firm. I was twenty-two, and in good health. I must appear and testify. A determination of guilt must be made, and that determination could involve me.

I remember the day, the room where the ceremony, or whatever it was called, was held. My father went with me; he was dressed in a dark gray suit and a blue tie, minutely figured. His eyeglasses sparkled. I wore a navy blue dress and trim coat, dark blue pumps, a small blue hat. There probably was a white collar, and my gloves would have been white. I was asked to tell what had happened "the night in question."

I looked at my father and at the lawyer who had accompanied us. I glanced at Gary Clark, who sat at one side of the room, looking very sober. He, too, was quietly and neatly dressed.

I said, "We took this short drive, and we stopped near one of the bridges in the park. Over the lagoon, but I don't think I could find it again. Not easily. Yes, I might have seen it before. When we were children, we used to take walks in the park."

"Please continue, Miss Fivecoat, about the night in question."

"Yes, sir. I — well, this boy — this man I was with." I kept my eyes down on my hands. "He got a little fresh — and Philip misunderstood — he'd followed us, you see. Anyway, he and Gary Clark fought — not for long — I had gone to the car — Philip's car — and from there I saw what happened. It was an accident! Philip lost his balance and fell over the rail . . ."

I didn't know how much of my story was believed. I told it the way it happened. And no charges were filed. Philip's death was called accidental. And I had done what the lawyer had urged. I had not let myself say that I was to blame. Though I felt that I was.

Another thing that comes up clearly in my memory — these events have no sequence for me — maybe Uncle Doc came to see me before the inquest, maybe afterward. Anyway, he did come, and he didn't say much or expect me to talk. He just held me comfortingly, and I think he was comforted, too.

I remember the funeral. It was private, but our family attended, staying together. We wore our church-going clothes, and there was organ music and the smell of flowers, and I sat numbly between Mother and Alice Peck, and I stared at the casket. Inside, I knew, was Philip. His red hair, and his familiar face — and I could scarcely breathe, knowing my own grief. And that of Uncle Doc, and Philip's mother, and Alan and Cynthia . . . This was all for Philip! For *Philip!*

During that time, I did not see the newspapers. Mother's little sitting room was turned over to me. I was not told to stay up there, but I did. I would gladly have hidden myself in a closet. I know — I knew then — that there was a great deal of publicity. The telephone rang constantly, and the doorbell. Hermann was constantly on duty in the lower hall. I would hear him say firmly, "The family cannot talk to you, sir."

It was a terrible time for all of us. I foresaw weeks and months stretching ahead of me when I would not leave the shelter of my home and of my family.

Mother could not talk to me without breaking down, and I begged Alice Peck to tell her she should not make the effort. But Father talked to me. He would come up to the sitting room and sit down in the chintz-covered armchair, and he would talk about the book I had been reading. At least, the book that lay open on the table beside me.

He talked about all sorts of things, the shrimp we had had for dinner, a new rose in the garden — and even about Philip's death. He knew that I blamed myself bitterly.

137

"It's not only that he was killed, Father," I told him. "But — Philip — he liked me. He always has liked me, and lately I think he hoped that he and I — But I didn't like him. Oh, I *liked* Philip. But I certainly had no plans to love him. And so I was cruel to him . . ."

"You can't possibly love every young man who admires you, Joey."

"I don't think I'll have that problem again," I said, feeling suffocated.

"Yes, I think you will. You are a very appealing young woman, my dear. You are small; men think you are fragile, and they want to protect you. You are exceedingly pretty — your large eyes, your pretty mouth — Yes, you will have to decide about other young men."

He was very kind, knowing what to talk to me about. He even talked about his work, recognizing, without mentioning, my interest in medicine. This was a great concession on his part, because I was sure he still felt, and strongly, that medicine was no field for women. But I truly believe that his talking to me about such things reached through to me and prevented my protective shield from hardening into a wall I probably would never have broken through.

I remember pretty clearly the evening

when I realized the gift which he was making. That evening — a soft summer rain was falling, and the smell of it on the flowers and plants in the garden below us came sweetly through the screened window.

I had gone down to supper that evening, but I went directly upstairs again. Father joined me quite soon, and he talked to me about ulcers. Peptic ulcers, of all things.

"They are very pesky, Joey, as you can guess. As well as painful. And if that isn't enough to afflict my patients, there is the psychological element. Nobody seems to want to hear about the sick man's ulcer, and certainly no one seems ready to show con- tinued and repeated interest.

"Just imagine bow Alice Peck would feel if she completed one of her paintings, and we didn't want to look at it or talk about it."

"We do, though. She's talented."

"Yes, I think she is. And in his way, an ulcer patient gets pretty talented, too."

I smiled, which pleased him. "They do!" he assured me.

Then he changed his means of approach. "You think I'm a surgeon, Joey . . ."

"I *know* you're a surgeon!"

"Yes. And you're right. I have the soft pink hands to confirm that." He spread his "soft pink hands" on the knees of his tan Italian silk trousers. And he smiled at me.

"But do you know, Joey," he said. "I consider one of my greatest successes lies in avoiding surgery for really bad ulcers."

"How do you do that?" I asked.

"Oh, it all began before you were born. I worked under a man, and since then I have continued to develop his therapy. I use concentrated predigested proteins. These first were used overseas to build up war-starved people. This man I worked under had fed hydrolysates to ulcer patients in preparation for operations. But he was surprised to realize that these patients were getting well without surgery.

"This accidental discovery led to research, in which I happened to become engaged in a small way. We already knew that ulcer patients needed protein to use up their excess stomach acids, and that many such patients were low on protein. This accounted, in part, for their run-down condition.

"We discovered that when fed the proteins every two hours, pain was reduced — often absent after several days — and within a few weeks an ulcer would not show on X-ray. Some patients even gained weight."

"You didn't need the Sippy diet then?" I asked.

His eyes brightened. "You've been doing some homework."

"Of course. I am interested in the work you do."

"Well, that's great. I'll bring all my problems to you."

I laughed a little.

"We do use the Sippy diet," he told me, "which, if maintained in all its gooey blandness, has much the same results. But it doesn't do much for blood protein, Joey. And the truth of the matter — the conclusion that I feel has to be made — is that either diet has a good psychological effect on the ulcer patient which, of course, is the most important factor in treating these people. Now I'll let you in on a secret. These moody, brooding ulcer patients show marked improvement when inoculated with distilled water!"

It was that evening that I, grateful for the help he was giving me, told him that I was not going back to the hospital as a Volunteer.

"You won't be asked to give that up, my dear."

"Maybe not. But I won't be doing it. Mother says she is going to teach me how to run a home like this one."

"Then you will be busy!" he said heartily.

He stood up. "I must spend a little time with my other girls," he reminded me.

I smiled and picked up my book. I even read a page or two.

I never saw Gary Clark again, or knew what had happened to him.

Of course this terrible, this tragic thing dampened the activities of the whole family. Alice Peck graduated from the Upper School and made plans to go to college in September. We tried to follow our usual routine. We went to Canada, to the Gaspé country, for our vacation. And when we came home, I again attended church and went out upon the street. Guests came to the house, and Uncle Doc did, though not so often. Mother, of course, never spoke up again in our defense, not even for Tread, whom she had often had to defend — or protect. But she naturally blamed herself for urging Father to let me to go the carnival.

I came to think, and then to know, that this was ridiculous. Gary Clark had been right. No one, really, was to blame for what had happened, one of us more than the other. I even tried to say this to Mother. She listened to me, stripping the lower leaves from some flowers which she was arranging.

"Yes, dear," she answered. "But — still, poor Philip is dead. I think of the young man he was, full of promise. And now there is no life for him, no hope."

And she, too, was right. I was sure that Uncle Doc felt that way, though he didn't ever talk to me about Philip. He was kind, always, and I wondered how he could be. I knew that he must hate me.

He showed his grief. All that summer, he was white-faced and grave. He kept working, and got recognition for his work on Paget's disease.

I wanted to go to the medical school library and read up on the disease. I knew, only vaguely, that it had to do with the weakness and developing deformity of bones, I ventured to ask my father if he had some material on the subject.

"Ask your Uncle Doc," he told me, brusquely for him.

"I don't think he likes me any more."

"Don't be hypersensitive, Joey. Of course he likes you. You've always been a favorite of his. Besides, he is mightily puffed up about his award. He loves to talk about it."

So, the next time Uncle Doc came to the house, I did ask him if he had some books or articles not too technical . . .

"I think you could take a few long-handled

words," he assured me. "What is it you want to know? Come and sit down."

He patted the couch cushion, so I sat beside him, and he talked to me about Paget's disease.

"The cause isn't known, really," he told me. "Except that we believe it is an imbalance between bone growth —" He looked at me, questioning.

I nodded. "Hardening."

"That's right! Between the bone hardening and the bone absorption, or softening. More lime is present at some times than at others. Ultimately bone growth takes over and exceeds absorption, leaving the structures enlarged and hardened."

"The legs . . ."

"And the head. Any bones, really. It comes on in middle age, usually."

"Calcium wouldn't help, or prevent . . . ?"

"Oh, it helps some. And Vitamin D. As for prevention, we never get the thing early enough, Joey. The trouble comes on gradually, and is well established before we know that his sore legs, or the fact that his hat no longer fits, means Paget. We doctors usually are the ones to discover the ailment while we are examining for other things."

"There's no pain," I mused.

"Well, not acute pain. And when one is

middle-aged, one becomes ready to accept an ache or so. Of course when the head swells a lot . . ."

"Does it really, Uncle Doc?"

"Oh, my, yes! Then the pressure can cause deafness, or vision problems — sometimes acute neuralgia. And of course I don't touch those things. But when the legs become acutely bowed, or the heavy head drops forward on the chest, then some bone surgery can help."

"And you do help! That's why they gave you the award."

"Well, I suppose so. It looks nice hanging beside the fireplace. You'll see it when you come out."

I sighed, and his arm strongly hugged my shoulders. "When are you going to apply for medical school?" he asked me.

I didn't have an answer then, but he had given me something to think about.

Uncle Doc was, really, a wonderful man. Perhaps he was bitter about what had happened through my foolishness, but he did not show it to me. Always he was sweet and kind. He brought me an armful of books and magazines about Paget's disease, and copies of some papers he had written. I still have them, and treasure them.

I have always thought it was he who sent Alan to me . . .

Alan appeared on our doorstep one summer morning and asked if he could come in; he had ridden into the city with Uncle Doc and planned to play tennis that afternoon. Could he bum us for a glass of cold water and a cool place to sit?

Alice Peck and I were glad to see him. We took him out to the garden and produced a pitcher of lemonade. "Even some sand cookies!" he cried in delight.

"Isn't that what you came for?" Alice asked him pertly.

"I should do something about my transparency," he drawled, stretching out his long legs. He was getting very tall, and he had the same handsome red hair which Philip had had. I wanted to touch it, but he would have had a fit.

He talked about all sorts of things. Was Tread entering med school? he asked.

"Not here," I said.

"And once in," Alice added, "we're not sure he'll ever get out."

"No," Alan agreed. "You couldn't ever call him the greasy-grind type. Is he at home?"

"Not just now. He's visiting some friends we know from Cape Cod."

"Are you going there this summer?"

We told about the Gaspé plans.

"That sounds great. Do you think I could tag along? Are you driving?"

I wished Alan could go with us. He was such a frank and open person. He always had been my favorite of the Winters.

"Would Uncle Doc let you go with us?" I asked him.

"I don't know. You see, Joey, he isn't one to let or not let us do things. He almost never passes out orders. The first time I remember was when he told me not to eat the rhubarb leaves."

We laughed. "Why would you want to eat them in the first place?" I asked.

"I don't know. Because I wasn't supposed to, I guess. But about Uncle Doc — that reminds me, Joey. I've wondered, these past weeks, if you thought he, or anyone, had asked old Philip to take you and, well, watch over you at the hospital carnival. Because no one did, Joey. That was entirely his own idea. And a pretty silly one, too, if you think about it. Because you can take care of yourself, can't you, Joey?"

I had been sure that my father had asked Philip . . . "I hope I can take care of myself," I said, my throat thick. "But I didn't do a very good job of it that night, did I?"

It was the first time we had talked about Philip and the carnival. The first time that we'd really been with any of the Winter family. Alan was being so matter-of-fact and natural . . . Of course that was his way.

"Philip was crazy about you," he said. "He always was, even when we all were just kids. I tried to tell him Alice Peck was prettier, but he wouldn't believe me."

Alice sniffed. "He knew an idiot when he heard one," she said. This made us all laugh again.

"The point I was trying to make," said Alan patiently, "is that old Philip wanted to think Joey needed protection. That was why he offered to take her to the carnival and watch out for her."

I had known he felt so, and it was quite possible that Philip had come around with his big-brother, bodyguard proposition. I had always resented his behaving so to me. Maybe that was why I had never liked him as much as I did Alan, who was much more realistic with Alice Peck and me. We were just children together, then adolescents, and only very recently young adults, at all times competing and communicating on a level of age and interest.

But the morning with Alan made me able to start out on our summer vacation with a lighter spirit. I realized, only then, that I had been blaming my parents for asking Philip to take care of me at the carnival, and I was heaping their guilt on top of my own. It helped to shed some of the load.

We enjoyed our vacation. The Gaspé Peninsula was beautiful, quaint, and cool. There were many things to do. I learned to sail a boat — not well, but well enough. I loved the water. I don't think girls were very pretty at that time. Our full skirts were worn at an awkward length, we rolled our front hair into nasty coils or horns on our temples. I never had dared to cut my hair. We wore heavy sweaters . . .

But we had fun. Even Tread seemed to enjoy the forests and the water.

When we returned home and Alice Peck went off to college, I determined to make some changes myself, to have fun, to learn to amuse myself. I worked on Junior League projects, and abandoned all thought of medical interests. I went to dances, and on select week ends with other young people of the city — our part of the city.

And before I really knew what was happening, I acquired a "beau." In our home, the word boyfriend was never used or thought about.

Ted Aldridge was a nice young man.

Blond, with lovely manners, but not at all the stuffed shirt Tread called him. His parents were friends of my parents, I'd known Ted in dancing school, he was two years older than I was. His father belonged to one of the oldest law firms in the city, and Ted was in his senior year at law school.

We went to art shows and to the symphony concerts together, to the debutante and Bachelor Club parties. It was fun to have your own special escort. I could see my mother planning wedding veils and silver patterns, but I knew this was premature. I enjoyed being with Ted, we liked the same books and plays . . .

I enjoyed, just as much, the short trips I took with my parents — to New York to shop and see the latest plays, to a medical meeting in Arizona . . .

But when I discovered that my parents were planning to go to the Bahamas for Christmas, I protested.

"Alice Peck doesn't want to make her debut . . ." Mother explained.

"But why can't we just have Christmas here at home, the way we always do? Here, and then out at the Village . . ."

"Dr. Winter hasn't mentioned it, Joey."

"He takes it for granted that we'll be there."

"I'll talk to your dear father. This year, he might think it wise not to go out to the Village. I am sure that is why he planned on the Bahamas. The sun, and the sea — You know you like that."

"Not for Christmas," I said stubbornly. Of course Mother was thinking of Philip, but — Our Christmases had become a ritual. Each thing done the same way every year. I wanted them kept that way. I wanted the pattern preserved of our beautiful, stylized Christmas tree, and the gifts below it. I wanted to go to church, then out to the Village where there would be the enormous tree with its familiar garlands and ornaments, used over and over each year. I wanted to be with the dogs and the people, to wade through the litter of paper and ribbons, to help clear it away. I wanted to explore my Christmas stocking, to find the orange and the apple, the nuts and the candy, and finally the very special gift for the year. I would miss the noise and the food, the crisp brown turkey and the crimson cranberries, the oyster scallop and the triumphant parade of the holly-decked pudding. I would not willingly give up the special joy of walking down the bridle path at dusk and looking back at the lighted homes.

I did not think I could bear missing those

things, even this year when the day could not, of course, be quite as gay, and when Philip would be missed so terribly.

I was swept up into a cloud of frustration, my life seemed entirely empty, and without promise for a future that would be any better. I could not study medicine. I could no longer work at the hospital. I could not even have the Christmas I loved.

I was so encased in this fog of disappointment that, to escape it, I wrote letters to Alice Peck about the way I felt, and even to Tread. Greatly to my relief and somewhat to my surprise, I found that they were rebellious, too. Of course in their own ways. Tread didn't want to leave his friends in the city, Alice Peck said it would be "ridiculous" to wear a bathing suit and heap our Christmas gifts under a palm tree. She, for one, just would not go!

We didn't really make a pact to behave so, but on Thanksgiving at dinner, always a rather formal meal — no, a *very* formal meal! — I found the courage to say to my parents that we really did not want to go to the Bahamas for Christmas.

My mother drew in her breath sharply and pressed her napkin to her lips. Father rested his knife and fork on the edge of his plate and looked at each of us in turn.

"By 'we,' Joey," he asked, "do you mean your brother and sister?"

"We all feel the same way," said Alice Peck quickly.

"Me, too," mumbled Tread. Alone, he never in the world would have voiced his objection. He was not one to communicate easily and fully with the family members, though I knew he could be talkative with his friends.

Father shook his head. "Well, dear me," he said. "Your mother and I felt that the trip would be a welcome change. . . ."

"We don't want changes," said Alice Peck and I in unison.

"We want to do things the way we always have done them," I added.

"Well . . ." said Father. "If that really is the way you feel . . . Of course we planned the trip for your enjoyment. But I shall busily spend tomorrow canceling all our plans." He picked up his fork and knife, and that was all that was ever said on the subject.

We did not go to the Bahamas. But we did not go out to Uncle Doc's, either. All our courageous protest had accomplished was our parents' return to their stiff and prim attitudes toward us, and toward a firmly regulated family behavior.

They loved us, but they wanted, above all

else, to be correct, and to see that we were correct.

I was older and my frustration allowed me to recognize and even judge their behavior. It was never discussed. But I had come to a point where I could analyze their stiff and proper ways as a means of withdrawal from everything that seemed vital, progressive, and possibly dangerous at times. It was as if we dwelt, figuratively, of course, in the bomb shelter which had been built in our garden, rather than risk having a brick crash through one of the front windows of the house, perhaps to injure one of us, perhaps only to come to rest on our pale carpet, having scarred a tabletop, knocked over a vase of carefully arranged flowers, and broken the delicate Doulton figurine.

Out of protest which I now realize was normal in a young woman of my age who felt she was being denied so many vital things, out of boredom which I entirely recognized, even then, for what it was, that winter I let myself become engaged to marry young Ted Aldridge.

It was not a matter of an overwhelming and joyous surrender to love. I liked Ted. For months we had been seeing a lot of each other; many of my contemporaries were being married. That spring, almost every Saturday afternoon was devoted to attendance at some wedding, either as a guest, or, four or five times, as a member of the wedding party. Our friends acknowledged Ted's interest in me, and my response, so we were always invited together. He wanted to give me a ring, and I demurred only until he said the proper things to my parents.

I expected to marry him, I made vague plans for our home, even for a family . . .

When Ted did speak to my parents, I thought they seemed more relieved than anything else. Of course they said the correct things, they kissed me, Mother got a little tearful when she kissed Ted. But almost at once they were asking us to wait until Ted finished law school.

"We need Joey here at home for a time," said Mother.

The ring could wait . . . the engagement would not be announced just yet. Long engagements no longer were the social custom; their thought was that we should wait until the following spring or summer.

And after a couple of months, I was not too surprised to decide that I could not go through any marriage with Ted. Oh, yes, I did like him.

"I thought you loved him, Joey," said

Mother reproachfully.

"I don't know much about love, Mother. I suppose I could have married him, and that we could have made an acceptable life together. A pretty apartment, then a nice house — a couple of children. But — well —"

Mother shook her head. "Does he know how you feel, Joey?" she asked.

"I'll tell him tonight."

"It will be hard on him. He is very fond of you. These rejections hurt a man."

"I am sorry . . ."

"But, darling . . ."

"Mother, I am sorry, but I have to consider myself, too. It is, as you and Father must know, time I was leading my own life, not dependent on you or transferring that dependence to a young man like Ted. And while we're on the subject, which I can see hurts you both, I think it is time that Tread and Alice Peck were leading their own lives, too."

Now they were shocked! Mother sat back in her small armchair, and Father actually turned a little pale. "We thought," he said, "that 'your own life,' dear Joey, was the one you were leading. That you now are living."

I was beginning to tremble. The palms of my hands were damp. "No," I said staunchly. "The life we three lead is not our

156

own. It is a life out of a book of etiquette, or maybe even Spock, but it is not realistic, Father. Not entirely, I am sure, and maybe it is not realistic at all."

I hurt them. I shocked them, and I was sorry. But I stayed with my decision. The next day, I went to the shop in the hotel and had my hair cut like a boy's. It was becoming to me, and I took courage from that revelation.

Chapter 7

For the rest of that winter, into the early days of spring, I would catch my father looking at me strangely — as if he were seeing me for the first time. I thought it had something to do with my hair, and finally I said something of the sort to him. I had come in from my day of serving as waitress at the Women's Exchange tearoom, and I was tired, as usual, and not as careful as I generally tried to be. I had my folded green apron over my arm, and I was detaching my nameplate from my blouse when I looked up and saw that Father was watching me.

"Is something wrong?" I asked.

"With whom, Joey?" he asked, in his precise manner.

"You were looking at me — lately you have been looking at me — as if I were a stranger. Is it because of my hair?"

He smiled at me. "I told you when you cut it that I regretted the loss of your golden locks."

"Yes, I know you did. But it is such fine hair, and —"

"We accepted your decision, your mother and I. We told you so at the time. Your mother thinks this new way shows off your eyes, your dark lashes and brows, to better advantage."

This surprised me. "I must clean up," I said awkwardly, running up the stairs.

He stood where he was, watching me.

I took a quick shower and put on fresh clothes — a slim dress of lavender linen, with pretty shoes. This was a gesture of apology to my parents; I myself had not been entirely enjoying my new independence, if it could be called that.

Dinner was as usual, the table prettily set, the food delicious. We talked of various things, the new curate at the church; he had come to call that afternoon.

"He hopes you can be of some help to him, Joey," Mother said. "He wants to set up a tutoring program for the high school students who fall behind."

I shrugged. "Maybe I could do something," I agreed.

We talked a little about the spring break when Alice Peck and Tread would be at home. No mention was made of our taking a trip, and I was glad.

Coffee was served in the library, and Father reported that it had begun to rain. He moved restlessly about the room, and Mother watched him anxiously.

"Do you have plans for the evening, Joey?" he asked once.

I shook my head. Then — "No, Father," I remembered to say. Those little courtesies were good things. I had no wish to abandon them.

Finally he came and sat down on the couch, but not in a relaxed way. He accepted a cup of fresh coffee, put it on the table beside him, then sat forward, his hands between his knees. They were tightly clasped.

"Joey . . ." he said. "I have perhaps been acting strangely these later days."

I looked up. "Not strangely, Father."

"What then?"

"Well, preoccupied, perhaps."

"Yes, that would say it. I don't want you to think I have forgotten what you said last winter, when Treadway and Alice Peck seemed to agree that we had been too restrictive on our children. Since, I should have been discussing the matter with you . . ."

I felt uncomfortable. Unhappy. "Father . . ." I began.

He smiled at me, and sat back, took up his coffee cup. It was translucent, one could see the shadow of its contents. "Yes, we do have things to discuss, my dear. But I have

160

been preoccupied lately with other things, namely some research which I have been doing. Such interests have a way of filling my mind."

"As well they should," said Mother quickly. She was always ready to defend my father's profession, to insist on its prime importance in the family's life.

Father smiled at her, then he turned again to me. "One of my lines of research," he said. "Of course I always have several in progress, because one must wait on developments, controls, and things like that. Do you understand, Joey?"

"Yes, Father, I do."

Mother had picked up her needlepoint.

"Fine. Then I can tell you that I have been making my own observations of an exciting new clue to the cause of stomach ulcers. Research on any level, in any direction, you know, Joey, is always being done, independently, by several men at once. This fact is both stimulating and, it can be, frustrating."

"To work hard on some development, only to have another man announce success sooner than you do," I agreed.

"That's it. Though we do try to be scientific and ready to rejoice when a problem is solved. By anyone."

"Has this happened to you, Father?" I asked. I was shaken by excitement. Father had never been one to discuss professional matters with me.

"I usually know when some other fellow is working along similar lines. Sometimes I even confer with him, or he does with me. On this work I have been doing, I knew that the enzyme which he called lysozyme had been discovered by Alexander Fleming. He's the penicillin chap, you know?"

My nod satisfied him.

"A great researcher," Father said. "Well, he discovered and named this particular enzyme; I knew that, and I have tried to get all the material I could on his work. He thought, and I think, that this particular enzyme destroys the stomach lining's protective mucus, and lays the stomach open to erosion by acids. And other digestive juices, as well."

He glanced at my mother. "Does this disturb you, my dear?" he asked.

She smiled and shook her head. "I don't really listen, dear."

Father and I both laughed. "Good!" said Father, and he turned back to me. "I have discovered that lysozyme is to be found in abnormal quantities in the stomachs of ulcer patients, and it is produced in enormous amounts when the patient is emotionally dis-

162

turbed. This enzyme, by the way, is also present in saliva and in tears. Well, anyway, my research and the purpose of it is to find some way to inhibit this troublesome enzyme."

"Have you found anything?"

"Well, not really. There is a sulfate — but, no, I have further work to do."

"I wish I could help . . ."

"Perhaps you can. Perhaps you can help me discover why four times as many men develop ulcers as do women."

"Do they?" I asked.

"They certainly do, Joey."

"Maybe because we cry more."

"Hmmmn. That has been considered."

"It would be." And we laughed together, which I liked.

"Release of emotional pressure," my father labeled my solution. "But this past winter, Joey, we have had a patient in the hospital who had a surgical hole in the stomach wall."

"Like the man —"

"St. Martin. Yes, somewhat like him. This hole was surgically made so the woman could be fed. She is twenty-one, and the measure had to be taken after she swallowed lye."

"Oh, *dear!*"

"But there is good in everything, because

it has let us observe the patient, and I found, Joey, that when Wanda gets angry or nervously upset, her stomach is quieter and secretes less gastric juice than when she is in her normal good spirits."

"But that's . . ."

He was pleased. "Yes. A direct reversal of the tightened-up way of men. Now — you tell me why."

It was fun to have him talk to me of his work; we both enjoyed it.

And then, within only a week or so — had he been testing me? — my father did a thing completely strange to him.

Alice Peck and Tread had come home for the spring vacation, and there had been the usual flurry of being glad to be together as a family, the long sessions of talk, of catching up. Mother insisted on a shopping expedition. Alice Peck consented, but Tread did not. He liked, he said, to buy his own clothes.

We girls pointed out that he always looked fine.

He did. He was a very handsome young man, dark-haired and tall.

Mother wondered if he properly considered the essential things — underwear, socks — enough shoes?

These primary matters were coped with, and the house settled down into a pleasant routine of more people there, of more talk, more music played, more telephone calls, and doorbells ringing.

But on the third evening — perhaps the fourth? — Father asked if he could have a full-scale family conference. It would not take long, should there be engagements for the evening.

Of course we all agreed. We could sit out in the garden, the evening was warm, and the roses were coming into bloom.

So we gathered. Mother brought a light wool shawl, and urged Alice not to sit on the ground — it could be damp. So she sat beside me on the bench, and before Father had talked very long, she held my hand in hers. She said afterward that doing so kept her from interrupting, from blurting out things . . .

And it helped me contain my own excitement.

I can, at any time, vividly recall the picture of that evening in the walled garden of our home. I can see the grass which grew in green ridges between the flagstones, I can smell the delicate perfume of the roses — red, pink, and one lovely white one, its petals faintly touched with pink. Alice Peck wore a light green dress with a white underblouse. I wore a brown skirt and lighter tan blouse. Tread had on light blue slacks, canvas shoes, and a white knitted shirt. Mother had soon wrapped her lavender shawl about her shoulders; she seemed nervous to me.

Father was, as always, carefully dressed. His suit that evening was dull blue, his shirt was white and his tie dark blue. His eyeglasses sparkled in the rays of the setting sun. It was that evening when I suspected that there was a dusting of silver through his golden hair.

But he was complete master of the "conference." We children knew that, on such occasions, we were to be told something, not consulted. At the conclusion, we might comment, but arguments seldom were heard, and certainly never were there objections. Alice Peck gave me a little one-sided smile in recognition of these rules as we prepared to listen to what Father had to say.

He surprised us. He really did.

Before he was through, Alice and I were clutching each other's hand until our knuckles were white.

Father began, seated in a chair, but soon he was on his feet, pacing the grass-rimmed flagstones.

He told us that he was blaming himself for

what must be considered the wasted year behind us. I heard myself gasp a little. Was he really going to mention Philip? I felt that old sickness crawl over me.

"A year ago," said Father, "I felt that I had thoughtfully arrived at the right conclusion, and based on that conclusion, I decided on the right things to do. I still consider that decision to have been right. Almost immediately, this was proven to be the case."

For a long minute he was silent. He walked down the path to the garage wall, paused there, then came back to us.

"Of course you know that I have been talking about the benefit carnival of last spring. Of the youthful, joyous occasion which turned into such black and stark disaster."

I shut my eyes to keep the tears from running down my cheeks. Alice held my hand very tightly. I was being swept with my great love for my father, and a renewed pity for him. He must really have suffered torments of regret on top of the natural grief for me, for Philip, and for all the others involved. He had known what was the right thing to do, and he had been persuaded to abandon the right —

Mother was weeping audibly, pressing her handkerchief to her eyes, her shoulders shaking under the shawl. Father went to her and stroked her hair. "I have told you many times, Christine," he said gently, "that I blame myself, and myself alone, for what happened."

My head snapped up. That was ridiculous! And I was ready to say so. Alice had persuaded Mother — Mother had persuaded Father — I had acted foolishly — Philip himself need not have followed Gary and me — I could have protected myself. It was not the first time a boy, a young man, had tried to force his attentions on me . . . I —

Alice kept me from springing to my feet and voicing my protest.

Father was speaking again, to all of us. "Since I was ready then to compromise my own standards, I feel that I now must be ready, I must be the one, to restore the normal life of our family."

What on earth was he talking about? What did he plan? It was my turn to squeeze Alice Peck's hand. Because now it was she who threatened to speak . . .

We both should wait and see what Father planned to say. Obviously he had thought out his speech.

"A normal life," he was saying, "as I conceive it, is one of chances taken, and happiness gained." He waited.

We stared at him, and then we broke up, each one of us. Mother wept again, I began to shake — after what he had said about the carnival!

Tread jumped to his feet and seemed about to speak, but Alice beat him to it. She dropped my hand and ran to Father, she hugged him and kissed him. "You are a perfectly wonderful father!" she cried. "So fair, and wise . . ."

He hugged her, smiled at her, and said something softly to her. Alice Peck was his favorite, I think. To him, often, she still was a baby. . . .

But now he told her to go back to the bench. "I think Joey needs someone to lean on," he said, his eyes smiling at me.

I did. Alice patted my knee. "There's more," she said softly.

Father, too, was recovering. He straightened his jacket and smoothed his hair with his hands. "Alice can be very vigorous," he said. "But I will not be diverted. I still have my plans for my family, and it is high time the first of these should be implemented."

I frowned. Now what?

But he was smiling at me. "I have been talking to Joey," he said in the friendliest tone one could imagine. "I have determined that her interest in medicine is still very much alive. So — it is my idea that she should enter medical school next fall. Provided, of course, that that is what she still wants to do."

I could not believe my ears! They rang a little with what I heard, and my head rang with what he was saying . . . but . . .

". . . can carry on her father's work. I shall help her all I can. . . .

"Later, I hope I can do as much for Treadway, and for Alice Peck. I would hope that their desires and ambitions would be creditable . . ."

I stopped listening. From that minute I paid little attention to anything. I forgot everything except entering medical school. I could do it. I would do it.

I did do it, that full. Father smoothed the way for me, and Uncle Doc did. He was delighted. "She loves it," he would tell everyone.

I did love it. Every minute, every detail.

Chapter 8

I became so absorbed in my medical studies
— the work was hard, as it is for any medical
student in a good school — the experiences
were traumatic. The sounds and the smells
of the emergency room, the long lonely hospital corridors at night, the meals missed
entirely, and the blotter taste of cafeteria
food — the many new friends I made, the
tremendously changed schedules of my daily
life — I had no time at all for the things that
used to preoccupy me.

Father watched me, a rather quizzical
smile on his face when I would encounter
him in some corridor. He called me Little
Doc, and I knew — now I can realize —
that the sight of me in my flat shoes, my
white jacket — a small girl with bobbing
yellow hair and big, dark eyes — was not
exactly the way his dreams had pictured his
older daughter, Joie.

Uncle Doc was different. He thoroughly
enjoyed my adventure. He talked to me, he
listened when I talked to him. I soon found
that he was the one to go to when any sort

of problem presented itself.

A professor who seemed ready to resent a staff doctor's daughter . . .

"Just brace yourself, Joey," Uncle Doc advised me. "You'll find nurses, even cleaning people, who think you're here on patronage. Just work hard and prove 'em wrong."

The first time I was called on to do a small demonstration in the anatomy lecture room — every student stomped his heavy shoes on the concrete benches as I made my way down to the desk.

"I hope you ignored 'em," said Uncle Doc.

"Well, I hope I did, too. But being a girl . . ."

"That's why they stomped. Such treatment, they think, establishes their male stompin' ground."

I grinned at his pun. "Next time . . ." I began.

"There won't be a next time. You were supposed to run screaming from the room. Since you didn't . . ."

"Thanks for explaining," I said. That was getting to be a stock phrase between us.

For him, I could interpret Cynthia's letters home. She was away at school, and used as much slang as she could when she wrote to him. I was sure she made an effort to shock her uncle. But I knew what she meant when she told of some girl bird-dogging; I knew what "made the scene" meant — things like that.

"Thanks for explaining," said Uncle Doc to me. "But what's happened to English?"

I was sure that Uncle Doc was completely interested in me and my new career, though even at the time I suspected that he gave me time because he was a little lonely. Alan was in Massachusetts studying law, and Cynthia was at school in Arizona. He welcomed a chance to talk to me, and I certainly took advantage of him.

He again came regularly to our house, sometimes only for a drink and a short visit, sometimes he would stay for dinner, and once, when the weather was very bad, he stayed overnight. I still would hang around to hear the two doctors talk, or argue, as the case might be.

There was an argument the stormy night when Father and he talked about the young people of the two families and their possible futures.

"If you would just relax, Paul!" Uncle Doc urged my father. "Let the kids find their own level. Sure, they may make mistakes. But the chances are just as good that they won't. The trouble with you, Paul, is that you are always avoiding, or seeking to flee, a danger not present, but one that you *fear* may happen!"

Father said something which I did not catch.

"Yes, you do, too!" cried Uncle Doc's hearty voice. "Go look at that fool bomb shelter you built in your back yard. And remember the imaginary trips to Switzerland and such places you took with your kids because you feared travel restrictions that never were imposed. You've kept your nice kids under your thumb because you had all sorts of imagined fears about what could happen to them. I hope you haven't made them permanently timid, Fivecoat, but I wouldn't bank on it."

This gave me something to think about, hard, that night instead of the lists of nerves I should have been memorizing.

The next morning, Uncle Doc and I walked through the snow to the medical complex; he had early surgery, I had a seven-thirty class.

I wanted to talk about this new aspect of my father, but instead I asked him about the surgery he would do. Later I was just as glad I had not talked about Father. I thought Uncle Doc was right, but I would not have been happy to seem disloyal.

Instead we talked about limb amputation,

the subject seeming to be not at all strange on that beautiful morning, with the city still quiet under its blanket of snow. The boulevard was cleared for traffic, but even at the hotel, the sidewalks were not all scraped clean. We both wore boots, heavy coats, and earmuffs.

And we talked about amputation and then about prosthetics, the false devices which were offered to the patients. "They never are as good as the original," Uncle Doc told me. "Especially for the hand and arm. Artificial legs do better, because there the main problem is weight-bearing, not dexterity."

"But you do encourage their use . . ."

"Well, of course I encourage their use. I insist on it. Do you know what my main argument is to these patients?"

"No-o. Pride, maybe?"

"Aggh, no! That takes care of itself, usually. Cosmetic reasons. No, sir, Joey, my main argument is to prove to the patient that no one ever makes full use of his available working capacity. Therefore, a patient who loses an arm or a leg can always still get along on what is left."

"That's good."

"Sure it's good. Hang on here, now, there's a glare of ice. If I slip, you hold me up."

I giggled. Uncle Doc would have out-weighed me by a hundred and fifty pounds.

"Another thing for you to remember, Joey," Uncle Doc told me when we had negotiated the icy stretch, "every patient facing an amputation stands ready to tell the doctor where to sever the limb."

"But you don't listen to him."

"Of course not. Because I place *my* decision on the place where an artificial limb will fit the best. And do you know? Even the patients who argue that they never will be able to use a prosthesis are the very ones who simply cannot wait for their tissues to heal and shrink. They want that artificial hand or leg clamped on at once."

"How long does it take?"

"That varies, but I hasten the process by applying elastic bandages, changed twice a day, and insisting on exercise."

"What about massage?"

"Never!" he said loudly. "You'd create tension on tender nerves. And now I'll tell you that six weeks at least is required before the limb is ready for a prosthesis. Here —"

He opened the heavy door, and I ducked under his arm.

"Thank you for explaining, Uncle Doc," I told him, as I started to run down the hall, taking off my earmuffs and scarf as I ran.

When I turned the corner, I saw him still at the door, removing his wrappings, but smiling after me.

He was a very kind man.

That year, without any discussion that I heard, our family went out to the Village and spent Christmas again with Uncle Doc. I was so happy to be there, and Alice Peck was. We scurried about like dogs returning to a familiar home; we checked on every detail, from kitchen to the top of the Christmas tree. Alice went out to the stable; I examined the bookshelves and found the new books and the old ones. My special Christmas gift was a thermometer and a slim pen-light; I kept patting the pocket where I had put the case for safekeeping. Dinner was as tremendous as always. The pudding blazed magnificently.

Alan was home, as much fun as ever, and Cynthia was there. She seemed to have grown up overnight, though she had always behaved older than her age.

She was a dark girl, with jet-black hair — she now wore it very long and straight, falling about her face from a center part. Her skin was naturally dark, and the Arizona sun had turned it the color of tanned leather. Her eyes were large, and I was sure she accented the heavy brows and added lashes.

Alice Peck and I didn't much like Cynthia, but she found, that Christmas, that she liked Tread. All that day, he followed her around like a puppy; he sat next to her at the dinner table where they talked softly to each other and laughed together about some funny thing not known to the rest of us.

After dinner, they disappeared, and when I went upstairs to get my coat, I found them on the window seat at the end of the hall, and they actually were petting. In the dim light I thought they seemed to be, and I was sure of it when Tread got so angry to realize that I had caught them. He accused me of "sneaking up on them."

I waved my hand at him. "Everyone to his own taste," I said, fetching my coat and going downstairs again.

I told Alan and Alice Peck that I believed Tread and Cynthia had developed a "thing."

"Don't worry about it," Alan advised me. "Holiday lasts only ten days."

Alice had persuaded us to ride with her, and we did, though I was terrified of horses, and my feet never would stay in the stirrups.

Anyway, we soon forgot all about Tread and glamorous Cynthia and their "thing." I didn't think about it again until the middle of the week when I went out into the garden behind our house to cut some ground-cover ivy for a flower arrangement Mother was making, and whom should I run into, coming out of the bomb shelter, but those two!

Tread looked as if he had been caught stealing sheep. We were not supposed to go into the shelter except in an emergency like an atomic bomb or a tornado warning, and I suppose my surprised face said so.

"Cynthia coaxed me to show it to her," Tread told me. His face had gone every color.

Cynthia laughed. "He didn't need much coaxing," she cooed.

"Don't tell Father," Tread called after me when I went on to cut the ivy. I didn't care how silly they got, but I knew the shelter was off limits and that my brother could get himself into hot water.

The next evening, Mother had arranged a small party — a dinner for several of Alice Peck's friends, with the rugs cleared, and a small orchestra for dancing afterward. Tread and I were supposed to be there, and Alan and Cynthia were invited, too.

It was a very nice party — pretty. I danced with Alan and with Father; I helped keep things going, and the punch glasses cleared away. When the "kids" began to leave, I helped Temperance in the kitchen and offered to carry some trash — napkins and things — out to the can.

"Where's Mr. Tread?" she asked me.

"Oh, he disappeared somewhere. He doesn't care much for girl parties." I went through the enclosed porch, and down the steps, and stopped. Our yard was kept lighted, and there, coming up out of that shelter again, were Cynthia and my brother. Tread's hair was mussed, and his shirt collar was up over his coat collar.

I rattled the pail lid, and they whirled, but Cynthia kept her arm around Tread's waist.

"You know you two are asking for trouble," I said to them, and hurried back into the house. I was confused. They'd been petting again; they had been away from the party for a good hour. Both Alan and I had missed them — and the shelter was still a forbidden place for us kids to "play."

Father had built it years before, during the time when a lot of people were concerned about atom bombs and the chance that some hostile country might use them to attack the United States. Certain areas were designated as disaster shelters, some people built them in their basements or close by their homes. One summer during our vacation trip, Father had had ours built.

Maybe the whole family knew he was planning to build it. I had overheard him talking to Uncle Doc about it, showing him the blueprints. He said Uncle Doc was welcome to use them for something of the sort out at the Village. But Uncle Doc said he was not at all interested in building a shelter. He pronounced the word "bomb" the way Churchill did. "Bum." Somehow they didn't sound so terrifying when the word was said so.

The two men talked about stocking ours. Father had lists . . .

"You'll have to restock it regularly," said Uncle Doc. "Especially medicines and the water supplies. They'll quickly deteriorate." I was still young enough that I had to run for the dictionary to understand the big words.

That evening I became a little bored over the lists of medicines, canned food, and emergency lighting fuel. But when the list moved on to books, my interest revived. I was up in the tree house; both Father and Uncle Doc could have seen me there. So I listened without any feeling of eavesdropping.

Father was telling that he was getting clear-print editions of the Bible, the complete works of Shakespeare . . .

"Aren't you providing some stuff for the kids?" asked Uncle Doc. "Seuss and Tony Sarg . . ."

"I figure someone will need to read aloud to the rest. There won't be much light."

"And you'll read *Shakespeare*?" shouted Uncle Doc. "The least you could do, Paul, would be to supply them, and yourself, too, with something interesting."

"Something like *Swiss Family Robinson*, I suppose?" asked Father stiffly.

"Something like Rudyard Kipling!" cried Uncle Doc. "Well written, variety, and lots of *stuff!* Good Lord, man, if you're going to bury your family in that grave . . ."

Father hushed him then, his glance indicating my presence. He didn't want me frightened.

I was not.

The shelter was built during that summer. When we returned from Cape Cod, or wherever we went that year, the garden had been torn up and then restored; it was difficult to see where the flagstones had been taken up or the work done. There were a couple of aluminum pipes and ventilators back under the shrubbery; that was all.

Within the first week, Father took us to see the shelter, showing us both the entry from the house and the one in the garden.

He showed us the bunk beds, and the supplies. I checked, and a lot of Kipling was there. Father talked to us children, explaining why the shelter had been built. He talked a little about war, and the need to defend and to protect oneself.

"We may never have to use this," he told us. "But it will always be ready if we do need it."

It was sometime later when he showed the completed shelter to Uncle Doc. That time I asked to go along, and I was allowed to do so. Uncle Doc looked at everything, tested various devices, especially the doors. "Be sure that Christine and Temperance know the principle of these counterbalances," he told Father. "They could get in here, remember, and not know how to get out."

"I'll be with them," said my father confidently, and, to me, comfortingly.

"You might be needed elsewhere," said Uncle Doc, going up the steps to the garden entrance. "You might be needed at the hospital, or be in the office when the bum explodes."

"If so, I shall be with my family as quickly as I can run to them," said Father.

"You'd leave the hospital . . . ?" asked Uncle Doc, his blue eyes round and wide. "Under disaster conditions . . . ?"

"Under disaster conditions," my father agreed. "I'll be with my family, or I shall get to them as quickly as I can."

They quarreled. Uncle Doc called Father names, and he shouted. Father turned very white, and he answered briefly, coldly. He scared me much worse than Uncle Doc did. I ran to the house, but I knew they were still quarreling. Not an argument, this time, but an ugly quarrel, the worst they had ever had.

I never went near the bomb shelter again, I never would have wanted to go into it.

But that Christmas holiday, Tread and Cynthia did. They knew they should not, and for all sorts of reasons. By then, I knew them all, and I knew that those reasons made the two of them find a way to talk to me privately.

They were together for that whole vacation, Cynthia usually driving to our house, or, as I suspected, arranging to meet Tread somewhere, at parties to which they were both invited, things like that. I don't know if they went into the bomb shelter again, and I didn't really care.

I suppose Tread — maybe it was Cynthia — worried for fear I would tell what they were up to. So they made a chance — they asked me to go for a walk on Sunday afternoon. Tread did, coming up to my room.

"I have studying to do," I objected.

"We won't be gone for more than an hour," he urged. "You like to walk."

"Is Alice Peck going?"

"Oh, she's just a pesky kid. Come on, Joey!"

"Who's *we?*"

"Cynthia and me."

I shook my head. "I don't like Cynthia."

"Now what way is that to talk?"

"She's as much a kid as Alice is."

But of course, in the end, I consented to walk with them; they must agree to get me home again in an hour.

I remember as we left that Alice Peck offered to go with us. I told her she was a pesky kid, and her eyes stared at me. "One of those, huh?" she said. "Be careful, Joey, dear."

She drawled the words, but I heard the warning. She didn't like Cynthia any better than I did.

"We're going only as far as the Art Museum and back," I told her, by way of an apology.

Tread wore a fur-collared coat that afternoon, and a fur cossack's cap tilted forward over his eye. He was handsome! Cynthia's coat was mouton, and the soft plushy fur looked rich on her. Beside their elegance, my tailored red coat looked schoolgirlish. I should not have been surprised to look down and see bobby socks peering out from under it.

It was a sunny day, but cold. We cut across to the park and struck out. I always had a strange feeling about the lagoon bridges, but that afternoon I had other things to think about. I can still remember how our black shadows followed us at an angle as we strode along.

As soon as we had reached the park itself, Cynthia urged Tread to "go on and tell her!"

I looked beyond Tread to see her face. "Tell me what?" I asked. Tread's cheeks were redder than the cold accounted for.

"Well," he said, "we know you're snooping around."

"She wasn't snooping, Tread, dear," Cynthia interrupted. "Joey wouldn't do that. But she has caught us a time or two — and, well, Joey, we want you to know that we weren't just making passes, because your brother and I have fallen really in love, Joey. We really have."

"You're only seventeen," I said, kicking a small piece of gravel with my shoe.

"Juliet was fourteen," said Cynthia, and I could have gagged on her syrupy tone.

"You don't seem much like Juliet," I said rudely.

"Why, Joey!" cried Tread, shaking my arm.

"Do *you* think she seems like Juliet?" I asked. They wanted something of me. I could wait for them to ask.

"She seems like a very beautiful young woman to me," said Tread solemnly.

I snorted. Mother would have been shocked. "You're both being silly," I said crossly.

"If you'd stayed in love with Ted Aldridge, and married him," said Cynthia, "you would understand us now."

I pulled free of her arm, and of Tread's. "You're not telling me . . . ?"

"That we plan to be married? Yes, we do mean that!" said Cynthia, moving close to Tread.

"But that's ridiculous, and you know it."

"When two people are in love, the way we are," said Cynthia, "marriage is what they want, and what their families want for them."

"Oh, certainly!" I said. "Tread's only finishing pre-med school. You're a freshman at your college. And you argue about being ridiculous? For instance, what will you two live on when you get married?"

"Our families make us allowances . . ." I think Cynthia said something about getting a job.

But I was walking on, thinking hard. I had been surprised to have them tell me that they were lovers, even shocked at the idea. Tread, to my knowledge, had never shown any interest in girls. Certainly not in one girl. Only in dancing class, or at the debut parties he was pushed into attending — against his will, as I remembered — had I ever seen him with girls at all. I knew of none that he dated.

Of course, maybe when he was away at college, though I had not heard him speak of proms or dates, and things. Even boy friends — I could remember only one. A year ago he had brought this southern boy home with him for part of Easter vacation. The young man had been equally interested in books, music and science. They spent practically every minute together up in Tread's room on the third floor. Playing billiards, they explained one time.

But now, here was this same brother, making out — she called it that — with Cynthia, and she could hardly keep her hands off him.

Now they were urging me to keep the affair quiet. Not to tell anyone. "We want to keep it to ourselves for a while," she coaxed me. "Please promise?"

It was none of my affair, and I told them so. I believed the attachment would blow away, once they were through the holidays and back at school. So I promised. "I never like to talk about silly things," I said grudgingly.

Of course, after that, I kept my eye on Tread and Cynthia. And I saw the romance develop to the point where I thought no "secret" would need to be kept. They were meeting each other at places other than our home, or out in the Village. I once saw them coming out of the hotel; that really troubled me, but I decided that they had gone to the coffee shop for a sandwich, or to the bar to dance. Tread was of age, and Cynthia got herself up to look as old. I kept telling myself that the whole affair was none of my business.

But I continued to watch them, and, ashamed of my thoughts, I decided that what Alice Peck called the "mushy business" was Cynthia's idea more than it was Tread's. Tread was nice to her, sweet, in fact. But he vas that way to everyone.

Cynthia, however, pressed. She telephoned to Tread, she made the plans. It was she who caught hold of his hand when they walked down the street, or snuggled against him when he drove her somewhere in the car, which Mother let him use during his vacation. Tread was Mother's favorite.

My parents evidently did not realize what was going on. Mother just said things contentedly about Treadway's having a good vacation this Christmas.

Though I kept my promise not to talk about the romance, or whatever it was — I think Cynthia would have liked to hear it called an affair — I thought secrecy was unnecessary, and certainly ridiculous. I didn't like the situation, and I wished I had not made the promise. Without it, I would not have talked, except to Alice Peck, perhaps.

I was certainly glad when my own classes started up and I didn't have to know what they were up to.

They were enjoying the secrecy as much as any part of their adventure. Whenever they were with either of the two families, or with the two families together — Mother and Father invited Uncle Doc, Alan and Mrs. Daly — Cynthia, of course — for New Year's dinner.

At such times, Cynthia and Tread were as prim as you please before the others, but they became very clever at catching each other for a swift, torrid encounter in the back hall . . . If Tread went up to his room to get some book to show Alan, Cynthia took the chance to go up to our bathroom on the second floor, though there was a powder room on the first, and of course she and Tread met on the stairs. . . .

When Father showed some films he'd taken the summer before, and the library was darkened, I was embarrassed, and aware, that Cynthia was snuggling against Tread there beyond me on the couch.

This angered me, there was something wrong about the whole situation, and I felt that I was being played for a fool. So when the pictures were over, I asked Cynthia to help me prepare a tray of cookies and milk — or something. I don't remember just what we were serving.

Anyway, I all but dragged her out to the kitchen. I refused to let Alice, or Tread and Alan, help, and I did it firmly enough to make them realize I meant it. Cynthia realized it, too.

"Is something wrong, Joey?" she asked me.

I counted napkins. "Yes, there is," I told her. "How many people are in there?" I knew. There were nine, with Cynthia.

She was waiting for me to say more, her pretty mouth was drawn into a thin line, and her eyes were cold.

"First," I said, "I want you and Tread to free me of the promise I made. Not to talk, I mean, about the silly things you and he are doing."

"It's more precious if we keep it secret," said Cynthia, purring slightly.

"Get down nine of those tall glasses," I said.

"Uncle Doc won't want milk!" she told me.

"Then he can get something else. But milk would be better before the drive out to the Village."

"Alan will drive."

"I'll bet he won't. Now, listen to me, Cynthia Winter!"

"Not if you're going to call Tread and me silly."

"Well, you are silly!" I was putting cookies on two plates, taking them from several tin boxes which Temperance kept in the pantry.

"Oh, dear, dear Joey!" said Cynthia, still purring. "You just don't want to grow up do you?"

"I do all right," I said crossly.

She was staring at me. "But — even though you were engaged for a time — you've never really *known* a man, have you?"

I dropped a cookie on the floor, I was so angry! And of course whatever else I found to say would do no good. She liked having a romance, whether it was serious or not. But unless Tread agreed, she said, she could not free me of my promise.

"But don't worry, Joey. Day after tomorrow, we'll all be going back to school, and at Easter, Tread and I plan to tell the families that we are going to be married next summer."

This frightened me, it sank me into despair, and it took a few days to realize that I really did not need to keep such a promise as I had made.

I would find a time to talk to Father. Then I would let him and Mother handle the awful situation.

A time came, and another time. But I said nothing. I couldn't talk about it, and I did not. Easter and even "next summer" would take care of themselves.

And they did. They certainly did!

In June, Cynthia and my brother were married. They had a big, beautiful wedding. I was constantly surprised at the way Uncle Doc went all out for that wedding. I even said a little something about being surprised at all the fuss he was letting himself in for.

"You never thought you'd see me puzzling about the merits of Mendelssohn and the

Trumpet Voluntary, did you, Joey?" he asked me. To my surprise, both he and my parents had seemed delighted by the match. Mrs. Daly said very little, but she seemed in agreement.

"I'll tell you, Joey," Uncle Doc said. "I haven't talked about it much, but I have a thought about this marriage which should please you as much as it has been pleasing me. Because I truly believe it is going to heal the hurt of Philip's death."

I stared at him. I could feel myself go cold. And before I could faint, or even say the wrong thing, I turned and ran out of the room.

The preparations went on. I was to be maid of honor, though I did not want to be. When I said so to Mother, she put her arm around me. "Cynthia has no sisters, dear."

"What has that to do with . . . ?"

"She's asked you, she wants you."

"What about what *I* want? I don't *like* Cynthia, Mother."

"Oh, yes, you do. Of course. And if you are a little jealous, darling, do make an effort not to show it."

I gasped. Me? Jealous of Cynthia? That feeling was not among all my emotions! It certainly was not.

So I was maid of honor. I could not attend

the showers and the luncheons and the teas — I was busy at school. But I was the maid of honor at the wedding; I wore a wide-brimmed hat, and a long, pale yellow chiffon gown; I carried a Colonial bouquet of daisies and delphinium. There were six bridesmaids in yellow-dotted, ruffled Swiss. Alice Peck was not one of them.

She had had better luck when she staunchly refused to serve. "I'd feel like a fool!" she said. And Mother listened to her.

After the ceremony, there was a large, beautiful reception out at Uncle Doc's. Two rooms were filled with wedding gifts, sparkling and twinkling. I escaped from the receiving line as soon as I could, and spent a half hour sitting on the arm of Uncle Doc's chair, listening to him and three other staff doctors plan and talk about the rehabilitation center they were going to establish, renting the rest of the building where Uncle Doc and my father already had their offices. This was a tremendous project, one of the doctors warned.

"We can swing it," said Uncle Doc. "We have the funds to establish the thing, and once it gets going, grants will come."

"If you say so, Dick," said the older doctor in the group, laughing. "I am afraid you'll get so enthralled with rehabilitation that you'll not have time or interest in surgery."

"The years will take care of that," said Uncle Doc. "Very few surgeons should use the knife after they are sixty. Certainly not after they are sixty-five. And I am getting there, my friends. I am getting there."

This shocked me. I never thought of his getting old. To me he was as young, as alert, as he had been all through my childhood.

The prospect did not seem to bother him. He talked with pleased animation about the crippled people who could not be cured, but could learn to use what they had, to get up and walk after years in bed.

Someone mentioned miracles.

"Miracles, hell!" cried Uncle Doc vigorously. "It will take hard work, and more hard work. On the part of the patients, I mean. But some will make it, and that 'some' make the whole project worthwhile."

The men talked of equipment, and the space needed. They decided that they would need some in-patient rooms and beds . . . Oh, they would need so much! But above all, they would need patients with hope and courage to do what would be necessary to bring them back again into the current of life. Surely, there would be failures. What bold venture did not expect that? But over all — to see an injured girl, a paraplegic after a car accident, learn to crutch-walk, to save life and living for the dozens, the scores, of injured people who could not be cured, but who could learn to live usefully with their handicap . . .

This enthusiastic, happy group was disbanded when word came that the bride and groom were ready to leave.

Uncle Doc grabbed my hand. "I forgot there was a wedding, didn't you, Joey?" he cried, leading me out to the wide front hall.

Alice Peck caught the bouquet, and everyone laughed merrily. She sniffed and tossed the heavy thing on a chair. "Cynthia will never make pitcher for the Yankees," she said dryly, and everyone laughed again.

So — it was over. We went home, and Mother hung my dress in the guest room closet, mentioning the cleaner. "You may want to save it, Joey."

I was sure that I would not. But I said nothing. If the wedding was going to bring our two families together, I would be as happy as anyone.

Chapter 9

It was an open secret that the honeymoon was to be spent at Sea Island. I supposed it was. I only *know* that, less than a week after the wedding, we heard that Cynthia had come back to the Village, alone from the honeymoon, and the next day Tread showed up on our doorstep.

He looked terrible, his clothes disheveled, his eyes . . . his face . . .

The family was waiting for dinner to be announced; Father went quickly to Tread. We all thought he was ill, perhaps had wrecked his car, a wedding gift.

I could not hear what he said to Father, but they went at once back to the library and closed the door. Mother told Hermann to have dinner held, and we women sat uneasily, not saying much, until Father came out of the library. He looked very upset, but refused to say anything until after we had eaten. I think Tread went upstairs, and probably a tray was sent up to him.

"No," Father told us. "He has not been hurt . . ."

Looking back, I do not see how we managed to eat any dinner at all, we were so concerned. Once Alice spoke up to say she had heard that Cynthia already had returned to her home.

"We'll wait, dear," said Mother quietly. "Your dear father will tell us."

That awful meal was finally finished; pure discipline made us go through the motions.

Then we went upstairs to the little bay-windowed sitting room where Mother conducted the business of running the home, sewed, or read. This was a pretty room with chintz-covered chairs, family portraits on the walls, the windows filled with growing plants.

Alice Peck and I sat on the loveseat. Mother sat in her low rocker, Father stood before the marble fireplace.

He glanced at Alice, then said that Cynthia had indeed come home. She flew home last night. Tread drove the car back.

"What did he do to her?" Alice Peck blurted.

"What did *she* do?" I asked quickly.

Father looked at us, and his face was very sad. "I asked Treadway both questions," he said.

"She was the one to insist on their getting married!" I cried.

"Joey . . ." Mother protested.

"Well, I know what I am talking about," I insisted, and I went on to say some pretty wild things. "She chased him, she really did! I caught them last Christmas, and they made me promise not to tell. Well, now she's been married, and she doesn't like it, so she comes home . . ."

"Darling, wait," said Mother. "We must be calm about this. At least, I mean, we must be loyal and loving to your brother."

"I am being loyal, Mother! That's why I am telling you . . ." I glanced at Father. "Now that spoiled girl has shamed Tread . . ."

He sighed. "Something dreadful has happened," he agreed. "I tried to persuade him to go out to the Village with me, and all of us talk things out. But he would not agree. I'm afraid he just wept. And by now, I am afraid he has left the house again."

This is where we were — a sad, puzzled, fearful little group — when Uncle Doc came storming into the house. We heard his insistent ringing of the doorbell, we heard his loud voice saying, Yes! He wanted to see Dr. Fivecoat! He most certainly did!

Father told us women to stay where we were, but I stood up. "You said we were to act as a family, loyal to Tread," I reminded him. "Well, can't we start doing that now?"

200

"Joey . . ." Mother protested softly.

"I know dear Father will talk to Uncle Doc," I cried. "Dear Father will shut us away from what must be a pretty ugly story. But I don't want that, Mother. Alice Peck does not. We are grown. I am a medical student . . ."

Father looked at us helplessly. "I would tell you Joey," he offered.

"You would tell us part of it," I said firmly. It was the first actual rebellion I had ever ventured. Sheer excitement, maybe fear, forced me through this one.

Uncle Doc stared, unbelieving, when we all came down the stairs together.

"I have things to say to you, Paul!" he cried roughly. "The woman . . ."

"We are a family, Dick," said Father.

"Well, I hope you are not all alike!" cried Uncle Doc. "That pansy boy of yours has sure played hell with *my* family!"

I understood the term, Mother most certainly did not. It turned Father's usually ruddy cheeks stone white.

His back stiff, he led the way to the library, saw us all file in, then he closed the door. "Now, Dick," he said, "perhaps you can tell us a little more quietly . . ."

"I'll never tell this story quietly!" cried

Uncle Doc. He refused to sit down, though Father did, carefully arranging the drape of his trouser leg above his ankle and shoe.

"Is that boy here?" Uncle Doc demanded. "Tread?"

"He came home," said Father. "He may be up in his room. If he went out, he'll be back. If you want to see him . . ."

"Better keep him out of my sight," cried Uncle Doc. "I'd break his bones . . . Did he tell you what he did to our girl?"

"I would like to hear her story," said Father.

"You're going to! You're going to!" Uncle Doc made a circle of the rug. Father sat in the desk chair, turned toward us. Mother and Alice and I sat on the couch; we were holding hands. Uncle Doc paced around blurting out phrases — he said something about cold showers, and wondered what good they did! — I had a wild wish to be anywhere but in that room just then! And yet . . .

"I'm sure glad Cynthia didn't come," Alice whispered to me.

I stared at her. And I began to shiver. "Oh, Alice . . ." I breathed.

"He believes every word she's told him."

Yes. Uncle Doc did. And then, we had to believe it, too.

Uncle Doc finally came to a stand before the fireplace, and he told us in short, angry sentences. I had never seen him so vigorously enraged . . .

"They were married, right?" he demanded. "They were married. Organ, flowers, church. The works. A week ago we watched them drive off in the car you gave them. They got as far as Louisville the first night. They went to the hotel — bridal suite, champagne. The works there, too. Cynthia dolls herself out in the kimono, or peignoir, or whatever it is called. The blushing bride."

Alice Peck snorted, but I hushed her.

"She awaited her bridegroom," said Uncle Doc. "And he never came. Not on their wedding night, he didn't. She waited, and she waited. She tried to locate Tread. Finally, at three in the morning, he called her. Seems he had this friend, this boy who lived in Louisville. Named Gene. Gene Lutzi, or some such."

Our three hands tightened on each other. Father took out his handkerchief and patted it against his face. Gene Lutzi was the boy, his school friend, who had visited Tread several months ago. The quiet, nice-mannered boy, interested in reading and science — he and Tread —

"Oh, no!" I cried aloud.

Uncle Doc looked at me. "Oh, yes, Joey!" he said. "There are a dozen names for your brother. Cynthia wouldn't believe it, either, but she saw . . . and she was told . . .

"Those two, Tread and Cynthia, never went to Sea Island. Tread spent four or five days in the apartment of his homo friend. Cynthia stayed in the bridal suite in a complete state of shock. Twice Tread came and talked to her. He said he had hoped it would work out. The marriage, he meant. He told her he could explain . . . but what was there to explain? She had no husband, she would never have a husband. So she came home."

And Tread had driven back to his home.

"She wanted to marry him," was the only attempt at an excuse that we made. I made.

Uncle Doc only gazed at me sadly. "I hope you will never understand, Joey," he said. And he left the house.

We just sat where we were, not able to rouse ourselves from the shock into which he had put us.

"I don't believe this," Father assured us. "When Tread comes home again, we'll hear his story."

Mother asked to be excused, and Father took her up to her room. Perhaps she understood what Uncle Doc had told us. Alice Peck and I only half comprehended the truth. In those days such things were not talked about. They were known, or guessed, but no one came out and said the ugly words explicitly.

I cannot tell you how long we sat there. Not talking very much, just comforting each other. Father, we hoped, would come down and talk to us. Once Alice said that maybe Tread would come in and tell us.

He did not.

Of course he didn't. Because after what could have been an hour, or a long fifteen minutes, the doorbell rang, and Hermann came back to the library, seeking Father.

"Who is it, Hermann?" I asked.

"It's a police officer, Miss Joey."

"Father is upstairs with Mother, who is feeling ill. I'll see what the policeman wants. If necessary, one of us will fetch him. Thank you, Hermann."

Alice went with me to the front hall. I cannot imagine the picture we two girls must have made to that closed-faced man who waited in our living room, an ordered place of green walls, green carpet, green damask couches set at right angles to each other — rose-striped chair cushions to match the bowl of roses on the glass-topped coffee table, and the rose satin linings of the green draperies.

Alice and I were wearing simple summer dresses, hers was blue, mine white. We were small, and young, girls; the evening already had put fright into our eyes.

"I need to see Dr. Fivecoat, miss," the policeman insisted.

"He is with our mother, who felt ill. I am his daughter. We are both — daughters."

"Yes, ma'am. But you see — there's been . . ."

"An accident?" I asked sharply, instantly thinking of Tread.

"Well, not really, ma'am. But — well, you see — this young man shot himself on the Lexington Bridge over in the park, and the papers in his pocket say . . ."

I sat down suddenly on the couch. *Tread!* Shot? On the same bridge where Philip . . .

I felt sick all over, and the next minutes are a blur to me. Alice kept her head, and the policeman went back to find Hermann. Father came. . . .

Even Mother came downstairs. But I lay there on the couch, my cheek against the pale pink silk pillow and the dark green velvet one, and I watched people move about. Their voices hurt my head, which was a buzz of pain and protest. Oh, no! Not Tread! I moaned, "Not Tread. *Not Tread!*"

Father was arguing about notifying Cynthia. Yes! They were married, but she left him. . . .

He wanted to go to the bridge, to the park . . .

"You'll have to go downtown, Dr. Five-coat, to identify . . ."

I sat straight up. To the morgue? To iden-tify my *brother?* He can't," I cried. "He can't!"

But Cynthia was notified. I was indignant that she should have first right. She had no claim at all, as a wife, or as anyone, I de-clared.

"We can go out there and talk to her," the policeman offered.

Father thought that would be better.

But she did come to our house. I hated the sight of her. All prim and grieving. She had drawn her black hair back into a knot, and she wore a dark dress. She would have kissed us all. Only Mother permitted it. Alice Peck just stood and watched the show she put on.

"I never thought he would kill himself for me . . ." Cynthia sobbed.

I grasped her shoulder. "He didn't!" I cried harshly. "He loved my father and mother. He killed himself for their sake!"

She left then, with the policeman, and with Father, who went along to identify the body. Alice and I helped Mother go to bed, and then we went to our room.

"Uncle Doc will come back . . ." said Alice.

"I wish he wouldn't."

But of course he did. Very early the next morning. Father had had the telephone switched off; he gave orders that we would see no one.

But of course there were people he *had* to see. These were kind people, sympathetic, and they all asked questions.

The rector of our church came, and Father must see him, talk to him, listen while the clergyman talked, offering comfort.

The coroner came, or perhaps it was just a man from the coroner's office. No inquest would be held, but there were certain questions . . .

"No offense, Dr. Fivecoat."

No offense, but hurt rubbed against raw hurt.

The undertaker came in person when Father refused to go to his establishment. "Do whatever you think is right," said Father.

But the man came to the house, a quietly dressed, quiet man of about thirty-five. There were certain details — which grave was to be opened in the family lot. Statistics must be given — Tread's age —

"His wife has referred us to you, sir."

"Yes, of course."

So Father must attend to those details.

The Hospital Center's Chief of Medical Services came, and he must be seen, talked to, his words of sympathy acknowledged.

Mother's wishes required Father and me to talk to the florist. We could have gone to his shop, down the block and across the street, but he came to the house. Father would not let Mother talk to him; she was in a state of near collapse, he said. But Father and I did try to tell him what she wanted.

"White flowers," she had said. White flowers all around Tread. Yes, in the coffin. And around it. On the top of it when it was closed. There would be no visitation, no funeral service. Father had had to specify those things to the earlier callers. But Mother was to have exactly what she wanted.

This last caller left Father in as bad a way as Mother.

And then, almost immediately, Father had to see Uncle Doc, though he tried to refuse.

But Uncle Doc came in anyway. "Don't blame Hermann," he told Father. "You knew I'd come. You knew there were things to be said between us."

Hearing his voice, loud in the lower hall,

Mother came downstairs again, her face white and drawn.

"Dick, please," she said. "Don't badger Paul. A man whose son . . ."

Uncle Doc shook his head in the way an animal does when he's been struck. "I'm sorry for Paul, Christine," he said. "I am sorry for this whole family. God, am I sorry for this whole mess!

"But now that you know what Tread was . . . Of course there will be a scandal. There always is around a suicide. Even a merciful one!"

Uncle Doc was a very angry man. It took me months to realize that most of his anger that day was not for Cynthia or what Tread had done to her, but because of the grief he was feeling, the deep tearing hurt because he was losing my father as a friend.

I had to leave the room — someone was really leaning on the doorbell and pounding. I went to the front hall to see if I could help Hermann. Temperance hysterically called that a man was climbing over the garden wall.

I telephoned the police and asked if we could not be protected from the reporters and the curious. They agreed to send help. I went back to the library to tell what I had done. As I came into the room, I was frightened at my father's appearance.

"I told you . . ." said Uncle Doc. "I did try to tell you, Paul. Last night."

Father sighed and nodded. "I didn't believe you," he said. "I thought — a silly girl —"

"But didn't you *know* what he was?" Uncle Doc demanded. "Didn't you guess? You are a doctor. This thing was developing right here in your home. You should have known! You should have protected our girl . . ."

Father jumped to his feet. He screamed at Uncle Doc, who shouted at him. They quarreled bitterly. We women were dreadfully frightened.

"*You* didn't know!" Father defended himself. "Why didn't you take care of your own girl?"

"Tread didn't live in my home. I never liked the boy; Philip and Alan didn't. He knew that, and he stayed away from us."

That was true. Tread never wanted to go out to the Village. Until last Christmas, when Cynthia . . .

Finally Uncle Doc left. Father sat desolate, and seemed scarcely able to handle the details that still came up to be handled. There would be no funeral, no visitation — he told that several times.

211

Yes, Mother could see her boy . . . We girls did not want to.

"Dick's right," Father would say softly to himself. Not to us. "I should have known."

That was when I formed my conclusion. It has strengthened since, but even then I was realizing that my father had been so busy painting a family portrait — mother, father, handsome son, two cute daughters — that he had not known, he had not guessed that he was using live people rather than crayons or oil paints. And now Tread's death had torn that picture, destroyed a large part of it.

I wanted to comfort, reassure him.

I regretted that I had not told him, last Christmas, of the way Cynthia pursued Tread, and had driven him into a corner.

He would not have believed me.

I could have had more luck telling Uncle Doc, about the bomb shelter, and all of it.

I had not told him. And I could not tell him now. The gap was too wide.

of course there was a scandal. A feature writer made a three-part spread of the Five-coats. In one section she dug up the material which had been printed when Philip was killed. For the first time, I read about myself in the daily newspaper, saw my Academy graduation picture in print; there even was a picture of our family and the Winter family attending Philip's burial. We looked like strangers seen in a newsreel.

And now they had this development. No mention was made of homosexuality. But Cynthia's wedding was described in detail. Again there were pictures — of the bridal couple leaving the church, of me again as maid of honor.

It was told that the bride had returned home within days, and the bridegroom, following her, had committed suicide. There was a picture of the bridge. Mention was made of the fact that Uncle Doc and Father were partners.

I wondered what they would do. Father, understandably, did not go to the office those days. He had a *locum,* he explained to me. I agreed that he could not work. My whole sympathy was with him, and with my mother. I was ashamed of my momentary collapse on the night when we first heard that Tread had shot himself.

When I said so, it was Alice who comforted me. Not mawkishly, but in her sensible, forthright way. "You'd been through the same thing when Philip was killed," she said. "You knew what would happen."

I said something about the whole family. . . .

"Not me," declared Alice Peck. "I was too dumb, both times, to understand, really, what was going on."

"Do you now?" Father asked her.

She nodded. "I think so. I know now that the whole thing — just about all of it — came about because of the way you and Mother have sheltered us. And other things can happen, because I know you still would shelter us."

"We loved you . . ." said poor Mother, who was really ill from grief and shock.

"Do you feel the same way, Joey?" Father asked me. "That we have been overprotective?"

I did, but I was not ready to speak in judgment. I loved them, and I said so. "That is enough," I said.

Later, when we were alone, I protested with Alice for saying what she had. "I wish you had not, dear."

"I think it may have done some good."

Perhaps it would. Perhaps it did.

Chapter 10

But it was hard to see any signs of this good. It was summer, the time of our usual vacation, and we went to Scandinavia. During those six weeks, I watched my parents build a shell about themselves, a shell which shut out Alice and me. She knew it, and said she was glad. I knew it, and grieved. I knew they loved me, but I was no longer "their child."

We returned to the city, Alice went back to her college, and Father told Mother and me that he was closing the tall house on Lockwood Terrace. Hermann and his wife would live there and care for the property.

He was leaving the city. Yes, he had already sold his practice and his office equipment, had resigned his staff positions. . . .

Mother probably knew about this, but I had not heard one word. During our travels, Father always claimed the mail.

I was stunned. What did he plan to do?

He said he was joining a clinic in California.

Oh, yes, certainly they would have a home. I was greatly troubled. I asked if he would like doing clinic work.

As things turned out, he did not like it. He disliked not being his own man. But that day he talked a great deal about new techniques. He was going to use, prove, and develop the use of a short transverse incision in closing perforated peptic ulcers.

He became quite enthusiastic about the matter, and talked technically to me.

"I've seen it used. I've used it myself, Joey! It has many advantages. The mortality rate, for one thing, is something like twelve per cent against the twenty-eight-plus per cent for a vertical right rectus incision. The latter is much more liable to wound disruption with evisceration, resulting too often in death."

I glanced at Mother. She had taken up her knitting. Father smiled at me.

"The general advantage of the transverse type of incision in abdominal surgery, Joey, is the conservation of the nerve and blood supply of the abdominal muscles."

I nodded. It would be.

"It preserves the fibers of the transversalis and the internal oblique muscles, both of which are severed in a vertical incision. The surgeon also has an easier approach to the ulcer, the patient knows a more comfortable convalescence, the wound closes more easily,

216

and hospitalization is shortened.

"You know, many patients develop severe wound infection following operations for peptic ulcer. When the short incision is used, evisceration or incisional hernia is not likely to occur even if disruption takes place. There is no need to visualize or handle the small bowel, and of course it follows that there is less danger of damaging it.

"Do you want clinical specifics?" He was looking kindly at me.

I nodded.

"All right! The skin incision is two and a half to three inches long. It is made transversely in the general direction of the fibers of the transversalis. It is started in the midline, about two inches below the costal border. If possible, always at or below the liver border. It is carried through the skin, the subcutaneous tissue and anterior fascia of the rectus muscle."

He was lecturing to me, a class of one.

"The right rectus muscle is pulled laterally, and the fibers of the transversalis are exposed and split transversely. A finger is inserted, and usually the ulcer is easily palpated. Most often it is felt to the right of the incision.

"You pick up the duodenum with a Babcock forceps and retract it to the left. The liver is elevated with a Deaver retractor. The surgeon, standing to the patient's left, now can look directly down on the perforation, which is easily closed by simple inversion."

It was a strange conversation, I realize now. At that time and place, following so immediately upon my father's earth-shaking announcement that he was moving entirely away from his work, his home, from the city . . . I had a thousand questions I wanted to ask.

But I listened to his lecture on ulcer surgery, and I took pleasure in the fact that my father could feel interest in something again. As he talked, now and then Mother would glance up at him and smile faintly. She, too, was pleased.

"Well!" he said then. "That's the sort of work I shall do in California. We want you to go with us, Joey. We hope you will do that."

And of course I said that I would. I was sorry for my parents, and I would share their new life. The next day I went to the medical school and withdrew as a student.

There really was no reason for me to do that; Father would have allowed me to continue. I might even have, in time, taken up again my relationship with Uncle Doc. I knew that he was fond of me.

There was no reason at all that I should not have resumed my medical studies in California. I just did not. The break with the past was to be a clean one.

We went to live in a new city, in a new home, and Father engaged upon an entirely new sort of practice. The city was big, its pace frenzied. I must learn to drive on the Freeways, to realize that one did not walk there. For exercise, one went to the beaches, to the desert, or to the mountains.

The home we adopted was certainly different. It was a low house, all on one floor, a spreading house with beautiful flowers, palm trees and strange shrubbery, wide lawns, and an encircling wall of adobe brick. I liked it, but I felt strange in it.

As for Father's practice — the clinic was a very large one, housed in a tall building of metal, glass and marble. The first time I saw it, an entire cloud bank was reflected in the windows of one wall of that building.

There was a certain excitement in these new things. I helped Mother get the home established. She had failed a great deal during the last year; her brown hair had a dusting of gray, and her eyes had lost their shine. But she dutifully set about making a home of the new place. I think it was when she discussed the decorating of the living room that I was shocked to realize that this new home was to be established exactly along the pattern of the old one. Wrought-iron grille, arched windows, or no, our new living room was to be green. Walls, thick carpet, damask couches. Pillows, chair seats and drapery linings of soft rose . . .

Gracious, quiet, self-contained, our home would again be stiff and proper. Beautiful, but cold. Proper, but not alive. I felt myself trapped within that adobe wall, and I knew panic.

Feeling smothered, desperately clutching at a life of my own, I went to the clinic and asked if I could serve there in any way. As an aide, or Volunteer — I had had experience.

The woman to whom I talked seemed agreeable, and took out a form. "Your name?" she asked.

"I am Joey Fivecoat. Miss . . ."

She looked up, frowning. "Fivecoat," she repeated. "It's an unusual name. We have a staff doctor here by that name. . . ."

"He is my father, yes." I watched her.

She put the form back into the drawer. She smiled at me. "I'm sorry," she said pleasantly. "We have a policy of not employing relatives of the staff."

Not even for free service . . .

Well, that was that. I would have to think of something else. Perhaps some other hospital. There was a large Veterans one only a short way — as western distances went — from our home. I would go there and ask.

But before I could do that, Mother found ways to keep me busy.

Several of her friends back home, it seemed, had written to friends that lived in this city and its surrounding towns. These women began to call on Mother. They invited her — "You and your daughter" — to a luncheon, to a style show at a club. They soon were asking her to subscribe to concerts — All this activity revived her spirits, and I was glad to see that happen. She put on a few pounds, and bought some clothes. Since she did not drive on these highways, I took her to the affairs, and it was simpler to accept the dual invitations. . . .

Of course, in this way, I met people of my own age. I was asked to do some church work, to join a study club, to do tutoring — and there were parties that did not include my parents. I even met a couple of men whom I liked. I went out with each of them to dinner, I played golf. . . .

Mother, in her turn, gave a party or two. . . .

This all kept me busy, after a fashion.

Though I still meant to do other sorts of things. I planned to talk about this to Alice Peck. She would certainly join us for Christmas.

Mother also thought she would come, and she began to make plans.

She would give a party, she said, to introduce Alice to our new friends. . . .

"You certainly are not planning a debut party," I said idly. "Not out here."

Mother was frowning.

"Mother!" I cried. "You wouldn't!"

"Well, dear . . ."

"You had better ask Alice how she would feel. I think you should phone her. . . ."

"Oh, she wouldn't mind. Would she, Joey?"

"Yes, I think she would. So you should telephone to her, Mother."

I insisted, and Mother did call her that night. As I expected, Alice hooted at the idea of a formal party and a "lovely tulle dress, dear. Blue . . ."

From across the room, I could hear Alice's laughter. Then she said she didn't think she would even try to come home for Christmas. She just could not spend the time. She was bucking for really good grades in the finals which were coming up — and she had three books to read for a French lit course. . . .

Mother was dreadfully disappointed, of course, and I was. I had stored up so many things I wanted to talk to Alice about. Perhaps I could go to see her. Not for Christmas, but maybe for a day or two later. . . .

I had not mentioned this idea when we got a letter from Alice, written only days after Mother had talked to her. Mother read it first, frowning, as she had frowned when Alice used words like "buck" and "lit" over the telephone. She folded the letter and handed it to me. "I wish we need not show this to your dear father," she said.

I was startled. What on earth had Alice done? College students were going freaky, college girls were getting pregnant . . .

But all Alice had done was to qualify for an art scholarship which would take care of her tuition until she graduated. Father would not need to send her any more money; she would be on her own. Independent.

"Why, Mother, that's wonderful!" I cried.

"But, Joey — there is no *need*. We can pay for our daughter's education."

She missed the whole point, and so did Father.

"Why should she want to hurt us?" he asked when he had read the letter.

"She doesn't want to do that. It has never occurred to her that you would be hurt. And you should not be. You should be proud."

"Of her grades, you mean."

"And of her talent. But there's her ability to be independent, too. That's what is pleasing her. That's what she is thinking of. It's natural, Father. Isn't it?"

"Yes, I suppose it is. You evidently think we should let her go . . ."

"Of course you should."

I only wished I could be as strong, as sure. I envied Alice Peck. I knew that she was seeking, desperately, to break away from the family pattern, from the wall such as was surrounding me. I tried to say something of this in the letter which I wrote to her that evening.

Mother watched me as I did this. I half expected her to ask to see my letter, but of course she did not. But the next day — I had started to address some Christmas cards. And I decided to put a note in the one I would send to Uncle Doc. I did miss him so terribly!

So I wrote my note. I told him that we were well, and that I would be remembering the Christmases at the Village.

I sat thoughtful, remembering. I nibbled the end of my pen, and became drowned in memories. The smell of cedar and oranges, the thud of the horse Alice always rode, the way the sky would glow as we walked in the twilight. I remembered the way my cold cheeks would tingle, and the cup of Uncle Doc's big mittens thrown on the settee just inside the door. . . .

Mother was watching me. "Is anything wrong, Joey?" she asked me.

I jumped and glanced at her. "No," I said. "Nothing is wrong. I was sending a Christmas card to Uncle Doc and remembering all the Christmases we had spent at his house."

"Oh, dear," said Mother. "I don't believe your dear father would want you to do that, Joey," she said softly.

"He can't stop me from remembering!" I spoke almost angrily.

"I mean, he would not want you to send a card."

"I don't think he would tell me not to!" I cried, folding the note, putting it and the card into the thick white envelope, stamping it a lot more vigorously than was needed.

Of course Mother told Father what I had done. But I was right. Father said nothing to me about the card.

I continued to send a card and a note to Uncle Doc at Christmas each year, but I did not hear from him.

The next spring, Alice did "break away."

Completely. Again she wrote a letter to my parents. And in it she told them — and me — that she had married. "A big Swede," she called the man. His name was Per Andersson. "I met him in the supermarket," she wrote. "We fell in love between the prunes and the instant coffee."

This made me feel good. I knew that Alice was covering up her happiness. I was happy for her, just as Mother was heartbroken and Father furiously angry. He talked about the grocer's boy his daughter had married. He did not say "had to marry," but his tone implied as much.

However, Alice, in her letter, said that her husband's father was a rancher, and Per was going to be one. She was happy, Per adored her, "as I do him. We shall live on the ranch, but during the next year I plan to finish my college work, get my degree, and have a baby. Please come to see us. Colorado is beautiful."

I drifted off into a dream of snowcapped mountains, deep green valleys, aspens, and blue skies. Mother began to make lists and puzzle over how to word the announcements.

"I don't know where they were married, Joey. The name of the church, I mean."

"Alice Peck would tell you. But why

should you worry about announcements, dear?"

"Your father talks as if he fears she is not married at all."

"She is if she says she is. I never knew Alice to tell an untruth."

"No, I suppose not. But to be married — without announcements and gifts . . . Though I intend to see that she has a trousseau. The linens I've been collecting, certainly, and we'll give them their silver for our gift."

I could picture the display. Rows and rows of forks and spoons, silver trays and teapots, serving dishes . . . gleaming, beautiful, but — in a ranch house? Perhaps Per's father was a prosperous rancher. We did not know.

"Mother," I said, "why don't you ask Alice Peck what she wants for a wedding gift? What she needs."

"Joey . . . ?" Mother asked, troubled.

I went across to her and kissed her cheek. "I'm thinking first of Alice," I said. "Her happiness. Isn't that the way we do with any bride? Shouldn't you think first of her and what will make her happy?"

Mother sighed. "I suppose you're right, dear. But I do wish I — we — might have shared her wedding."

I wished so, too. I wanted to *see* Alice. I

wanted to go to see her, and perhaps learn her secret of building her own life. I could not go just then. But she would invite me, and then I would go.

For the time, I could try to do things that would make my life my own.

I did try.

I still think it was because of Alice that I gathered enough determination to get myself a job. I did that the first of the next week. I looked at the advertisements in Sunday's newspaper, and on Monday I applied for a position as receptionist, with some typing. I was hired at once.

Mother was somewhat dismayed. She said she would miss my help.

"Hire a gardener who can drive," I told her hardily. "The way Hermann used to drive you."

My position was in an office setup that reminded me of Father's and Uncle Doc's. These men were younger — there were three of them — an internist, an allergist, and a dermatologist. The ground-level office was built around a garden court. There were two nurses, two technologists, and a secretary. Now there was a receptionist. Me. And before the second week I was helping a little in the lab. I explained my scientific courses at college, but told no one about the year at medical school. I liked the lab work, and asked to be shown how to do other things.

"Why not learn?" asked the lab girl, a sensible, plain woman of forty. "I mean, go to school. Technologists get good pay."

So I did learn. I enrolled in evening classes, and handled my office work, too. Of course this meant that I was very busy. I considered getting a small apartment near the office, but I never did that.

I did buy my own clothes, and once I talked to Father about my idea of specializing in blood chemistry.

He listened courteously, made a few comments, then urged me to be careful out on the streets at night. He had given me a small car.

That year fairly flew by. And the next summer, being awarded a week's vacation, I went to see Alice Peck and her big Swede in Colorado. Her baby was a five-months-old darling, lying on a blanket in the sun, kicking his heels and chortling at me.

She was right. Per did adore Alice. She was so happy it hurt me. Her curly hair cut short, she wore jeans and white blouses, stout shoes. She looked wonderful.

The ranch was a horse ranch — or camp

— where a limited amount of visitors could come for vacations. They lived in small cabins, and luxury was the last consideration. In time, perhaps the Anderssons might develop a ski resort. . . . There were a couple of good slopes.

"I'll be your best customer," I assured Alice.

"We'd lose you in the first good snowfall," she teased me.

Alice looked wonderful, her skin brown, her blue eyes clear. I loved even the horses, which still terrified me. But the food — steaks, fresh vegetables, beans — often cooked and eaten out of doors — I had no reservations about that. The whole atmosphere of the place delighted me, the air like wine, the casual routine of our days, the loving warmth of that home.

I believed Alice was completely happy, and I told my parents that she was.

"And she certainly has not married a grocer boy," I added. "Mr. Andersson is a geologist, and lectures at the University, conducts research expeditions. Mrs. Andersson goes with him. Your grandson is beautiful. All of Alice's babies will be beautiful."

"I dare say they will have a large family."

"They named the first son Paul, you know."

"Yes. I have set up a trust fund."

"She would rather you'd go to see them, watch the baby fall asleep like a puppy in the sunshine. All of her children will be like that, as free as puppies, and as independent."

Father regarded me gravely. "Is that what you want, Joey?" he asked me wistfully.

"It will never be the same for me. But I would like for all of us to be happy, Father."

"And we have not been," he said wryly.

"I don't know, Father. Some terrible things have happened in our family."

"You think I failed you?"

"Not failed. Nor deprived us. You have given us so much. You've loved us children, and planned for us. We should have been happy."

"Weren't you? Ever?"

"Oh, yes, of course. We were happy many times. In many ways."

I sat thoughtful, watching the dark water of the little pool before our chairs on the patio. Goldfish darted among the plants.

"And yet . . ." Father prodded me.

I straightened in my chair. "Beauty and serenity . . . They have escaped us. The setting has been there. A beautiful home, gracious living. Your own elegance and prestige as a professional man . . ."

"But . . . ?" he asked, his tone brittle.

I didn't answer right away. I did not want to hurt him. I loved him and Mother, perhaps more than I had ever done in my life, but still I felt the only way was to be honest with them.

So when I did answer, I said slowly, "I've decided — I believe, Father, that life has to be lived, and not made into one of those dioramas they put into museums. To be looked at through a glass window. I know life can be grubby, and that that is what you sought to protect us from.

"But protection, ignorance, is not always the way to save one's children from hurt, or even contamination."

I was thinking of Tread, and the way of life he had learned under the canopy of strict parental supervision, carefully selected schools, and friends.

I was thinking of myself, and how little I was ready to protect myself, or use good judgment, when I should have been old enough to do both.

It hurt my father for me to talk as I had done. Frankness and honesty between us always made for hurt. He wanted to be right, he wanted to be proud, he wanted to maintain that image for the world, for his family, and for himself. My mother understood that need in him and she went loyally along with him. Out here in the new clinic, he was working hard. Sometimes the doctors in our office would say something about the work he was doing, and seem surprised that I knew nothing at all about it.

"He leaves his work behind in his office and o.r.," I would explain lamely.

"But you're interested in medicine . . ."

"He knows that. He doesn't think families should mix things up."

To that, no one commented.

And I was glad to have the subject dropped. I could have talked to Father — we had used to do it on rare occasions. It would have brought us more closely together than any other thing; it could have changed our lives if he would have let me work with him. But he would not permit any such thing. He did not want me to work at all. He said that I was all he had left, surely he could take care of me.

I would not give in to him. I suggested that we could share each other's interests. "I could tell you about the latest thing in centrifuges, and you could explain to me what all the fuss is about intestinal bypass."

He shook his head, smiling but firm. The nearest he ever came to discussing his professional life in my hearing was the evening that Mother gave one of her elegant small dinner parties. I had not expected to be at the table, but someone defected, and she asked me to fill in.

"I have a class, Mother."

"Just this one time, please, Joey. I do want this party to be perfect."

"I haven't a proper dress."

"But of course you have. I persuaded you to get that long white linen, remember?"

I had never worn it. I had no occasion to wear anything so sophisticated to the lab or to my classes. Anything so bare, either. Though I had maintained my tan, driving back and forth to the lab, and swimming on week ends. So I brushed my hair into a shining cap, I slithered into the white sheath, rubbed my hand over my bare shoulders, and knotted the long, brightly flowered scarf about my waist. And I appeared at the dinner.

There were twelve people — I sat between a judge of the federal court and a man who did something with documentary movies. The guests were handsome people, but none so handsome as my distinguished father, with his silvered, thick blond hair, his aquiline, high-colored face, and his ability to talk amusingly, wittily, about the children of today, as a doctor saw them, as the clinics and hospitals saw them.

234

It was a charming exposition. I was charmed.

He agreed that the health habits of children were faulty, he agreed that too much was done for children. They didn't know how to *walk!* But, he said, "The real problem we doctors face and do not always handle is the fact that children will swallow everything and anything."

Surprised, the guests laughed and leaned forward, anxious to hear more.

"Toy airplanes, teeth, safety pins, Sunday school buttons and military decorations — they are just a few of the indigestible things that children — and some adults — are constantly gulping. You'd be surprised at how large a percentage of the population owes its life to the bronchoscope and the surgeon's knife. Our clinic, on an average of one every four days, goes mining and recovers items euphemistically called 'foreign bodies.' You would recognize them as cuff links, coins, peanuts, seeds of all sorts from pumpkin to sunflower, hairpins, staples, toy automobiles, and a Kennedy button."

Laughter swept around the table, flickering the candles in the tall silver sticks, lifting the petals of the yellow roses on the mirrored centerpiece.

Yes, he was delightful. No one would have

235

wanted him to talk in technical terms at such a dinner party.

But, later, when I brought up the matter — we were out in the courtyard, or atrium, and were reading the Sunday paper — I wanted to change the subject from Mother's protest because I had not agreed to a date with the documentary film chap — so I asked Father if it was getting easier to recover his "foreign objects."

"The bronchoscope has about eliminated the dangers of infection," he said, and then he himself changed the topic of conversation. How would we like to go for a sail? he asked.

I went for the sail — I loved the water — and half the pleasure of living in California was the availability of such expeditions. But on that day of sun-sparkle, golden light and blue skies, the fresh breeze on my face, I was sternly asking myself what I was going to do. The months were sliding by, and I was accomplishing nothing. Not really. I still was giving first consideration to everything in the world except myself. And it was not selfish to want to build my own life! Father and Mother would make that claim, but it was *not* selfish!

I would hurt them by almost any move I would make away from them and their ideas of what I should properly do, so I might as well make a decision, make it a good one, and state it soon and definitely. Alice had shown me the way. She had left the family nest, the marsupial pouch, and she was happy.

Could I not do the same sort of thing? Marriage was not essential, though I might have managed even that, without leaving, but certainly not escaping Mother's flutterings and hoverings, the yellow organdy and the "Trumpet Voluntary."

So I decided. Even as I ducked and escaped being thrown into the water when Father came about, I decided that I would leave. I would go elsewhere, and find a job, and I would be happy!

"If it takes a leg and an eyebrow!" I said aloud.

"What did you say, Joey?" asked Father.

"Nothing really. Just humming a few words to myself."

So I would begin my new life by telling a fib.

Long before, while doing my brief medical studies, I had become inspired by the work being done even then in open heart surgery. My budding ambition had been to qualify for some work along that line.

During recent months, those of us who

worked in the doctors' offices had all come to know a child, a patient with allergies that were varied and difficult to handle. During the examinations and tests the little girl was put through, it was discovered that a heart irregularity was present. This of course was referred to the specialists, but we all were interested in the child, and in what was being done for her. This intensified our natural interest in the rapid development of open heart surgery. We would sit over coffee and talk about the doctors doing this work. Dr. Barnard became as familiar to us as if he were a member of the group. And we were excited to know of the work being done in the Texas clinics. Their work stirred my imagination as few things had ever done.

So, when I decided that I would go elsewhere, Texas became my chosen goal.

This was to be a clean break, a real one. It would be different from my getting a job while continuing to live in my father's home, my meals guaranteed, driving the car which he had given to me.

I did, however, take the car when I started on my adventure in independence. He asked me to take it; the car had been a gift. He also said that I could always come back, so I knew the car was a safety rope against my need to return. But I was pretty sure I would not come back, not to live, and that I would never again be a daughter of the house.

I had a little money saved, I had the income from a small trust fund left to me by my grandfather Peck. I would drive to Texas, I would find a job in or connected with one of the heart clinics; I now had experience in lab work, I knew how to wash test tubes, if nothing better offered.

The friends I had made at our office were both sorry and pleased to see me go.

"Come back and marry me, Joey," said the X-ray technologist.

"Oh, I am going to marry Dr. Cooley!" I assured him.

"He should be that lucky!"

So I departed on an excited, happy note, almost as if I knew what lay before me.

I reached Houston without any of the mishaps my mother had feared would befall me, a young woman alone in a car. I made inquiries and applied for a job, which I got. It was in one of the large clinics, and I was to do lab work with blood. My plan, as I recall, was perhaps to go into a nurse's training course, and specialize in the field of heart surgery, eventually becoming one of a team.

I found a small apartment, I made friends.

And I liked the work I was doing as an humble part of the great work being done in the clinic. I was intrigued by the patients who came to the clinic, the white-faced children, the fainting young mothers, the great men of the world stricken before their usefulness should have been ended. It was wonderful to see these same patients leave our clinic stronger, with good color, and a bright hope for the future.

And in Texas I found romance.

I found Michael.

A group of us had gone to New Mexico to ski over a long week end. Michael was there, and knew some of our group; he worked in Houston, but at another hospital where he was a resident surgeon, specializing in the care of cardiac children.

He was a big young man with flaming red hair, a kind face — a warm voice. He was a special person, his was a special name, his a special face. He made the air bright. Within a few hours I was in love with Michael.

That first evening we sat across the hearth from each other, warming ourselves before the leaping fire. Our eyes met, and he smiled at me. Almost at once he moved to sit on the rug before the couch where I sat. We ate our dinner there, having fetched laden plates from the buffet. We joined the others in the songs that were sung. We listened to, and shared in, the talk. Within an hour his head was back against my knee, and his hand held mine warmly, strongly.

And by midnight we found ourselves left alone before the fire, now falling into rosy coals. We talked — about a thousand things. Our childhood, our families — he had a mother who had married a second time, and lived a frenzied life.

"You don't?" I teased.

He chuckled. "All heart surgeons are egocentrics," he told me.

"Most *surgeons* are," I assured him.

He glanced up at me. "You aren't one?"

"Not me. But I have a father . . ."

We talked about my father, and about Uncle Doc. We argued a bit when we talked about the surgeons he worked with and knew. We discussed their talents as well, but not quite so thoroughly, as we discussed their faults and failings. We discussed our own faults and failings.

He could not endure stupidity, and he had a too-quick temper. "That's terrible for a children's doctor," he assured me.

I confessed that I was a coward.

"Big dogs, and revolving doors," he decided.

"And horses' big teeth," I agreed. "But,

seriously, I am most afraid of myself."

"How's that?"

"I am inclined to give in."

"To avoid a row," he decided.

"Yes. And whenever I get independent, I hurt somebody. So —"

"Good!" he told me. By then he was sitting beside me on the couch, my head in the hollow of his shoulder. Warm, and safe. "We won't ever let you be independent again," he promised.

Within another five minutes, we were both fast asleep.

Within a month we were married. Secretly.

We went back to New Mexico, and we were married by a priest friend of Michael's in an old, old mission church. The sky blazed blue above the mountains, the church was dusky with brown shadows, and smelled of wax. Our honeymoon consisted of the leisurely days it took us to drive back to Houston.

We didn't make any plans. It was enough to have found each other and to know love.

We would not tell anyone, just yet, of our marriage, we decided. I decided. I would continue to work at my job, I said.

"I'd be glad to have a working wife," Michael assured me.

I was the one who wanted to keep the

marriage secret. He didn't care. "I'm sure to do things to your reputation," he promised.

I tried to explain that my reason had to do with other unhappy times in the family because of other weddings.

"Do you want to tell me about it?" he asked.

"Sometime, yes. Yes, of course."

He let it go at that.

So our marriage was to be secret from my family. For a time. I thought the chance of shock would lessen with time. And, though I did not try to explain this to Michael, I wanted to hold and to keep this wonderful thing which was my own. For a time. And Michael said nothing to dissuade me.

We were happy just to belong to each other, to share the house we had found. We were happy in the work we did. "Until the first bouncing boy," Michael specified.

"If he takes after you, he'll bounce," I agreed. "Though if he is unlucky enough . . ."

"Little rubber balls bounce, too," he assured me. "You get better at it all the time."

I knew what he meant, and he was right. He was a very busy doctor, he worked hard, and studied a lot. But in our time together, we talked about everything, we played games — we became especially adept at backgammon. The hospital group warned each other not to play that game with Mike and Joey Broughton. Other games, just maybe. It was fine with us. Any game pleased us.

Our home life was fine. Michael liked things to be simple. And if he liked a thing, I did. We had just enough furniture to fill our needs. There was no crying call for thick carpets in southern Texas. An oak floor, well scrubbed and rubbed, was a pretty sight. His idea of a fine dinner was a good omelet, a fresh salad, crusty bread and good cheese.

Of course we were happy. And content, which was even better.

I continued to go regularly to see my parents, and to see Alice Peck.

She knew that I was married. "Is he good to you, Joey?" she asked.

"He — cherishes me, Alice P. He is the sort of man to cherish a thing he loves."

"I am so glad, Joey! So *glad!*"

When Michael went on staff, he urged me to go on and study medicine, but I decided that I would not. "Three babies would be better," I told him.

"As good an appraisal of the profession as I ever heard," he decided.

We found, bought, and moved into, a new house. We did the things we wanted to do with it. A stone fireplace, and windows from floor to ceiling. Then Alice Peck came to visit us. We all got along wonderfully well together. Per, Alice and her two children. My big husband with his steady eyes, his ringing voice.

"Why did you hesitate to show your family to me?" Michael asked me. "They are wonderful!"

Alice and I looked at each other. "I never . . ." I began. Then I started over. "Alice never worried me," I said.

"But your mother and father did," said Michael. "They do."

"She — You must tell Mother and Father, Joey," Alice told me.

"Yes. I plan to. They can't take this away from me now."

She smiled and shook her head. "You can't give it away now," she corrected.

I could not; I would not. And I would tell them, I promised.

Chapter 11

Michael's schedule was too heavy for us both to go to California that summer. He urged me to go alone, and to tell my parents. I said that I would, but I made no definite plans.

I thought there was time. My parents' life must be neatly, safely settled into its routine by now. There was no risk of any further upsets due to their children. . . .

Of course there was my marriage, but that was such an accomplished fact that it should cause no more than a ripple.

Alice scolded me because I had not yet told Mother and Father. "Who are you and Mike to escape all that silver?" she asked. "Not to mention the Madeira embroidered bun covers."

"I want Michael to go with me. . . ."

"He doesn't plan vacations the way Father did, does he?"

"No. He isn't much like Father in any way."

She agreed. "I get notice when they leave for Majorca or Scotland, don't you?"

"Yes, I do. I think they are quite comfortable, Alice, in their way of living."

"You'd still better write them or go home and tell them in person. . . ."

"You and Michael sing the same song," I told her. "Though you both know I am a coward."

"I know you are a coward, but I never thought you'd be selfish."

I had not quite recovered from that when Mother telephoned to me.

Her voice was shaken. She broke down once and cried. Yes, she said, there was trouble. "Your dear father . . ."

"Has something happened to Father?" I asked sharply.

That was when she cried. "Oh, not physically, Joey," she told me, sobbing. "But it is terrible, just the same. Can you come home . . . ?"

"Mother . . ."

"He wants you, Joey."

I was troubled — and frightened. Michael said of course I must go. No, his surgical schedule would not let him get away. . . .

I knew that. He was doing eight or nine surgicals a day.

I called for a plane reservation, I packed some clothes, getting more panicky by the minute. Just facing my parents was enough

— but if my father had collapsed in a way to frighten Mother . . .

I decided that another woman must have entered their lives. This was ridiculous, but *something* must have happened! What was I going to do? I was two years older than when I had left the shelter of their home, but I knew, once I entered it again, I would be twelve, and I would wait for my parents to make the decisions. Well, if that was going to be the case . . . Why had I come? I wanted to be at my own home, roasting a chicken for the week end, reading in bed until Michael came in from the hospital to tell me all about a case, to eat a sandwich, drink a tall glass of milk, take a hot bath, and come to bed, waking at dawn to draw me into his arms. . . .

When the plane landed, there was a message for me — I was "Miss Fivecoat" again — and a car was waiting to drive me to my parents' home. That home looked the same. Tiled roof, arched windows, gleaming stucco — palm trees, camellias — huge geraniums.

But inside, Mother came to meet me, and collapsed, weeping, in my arms. I looked beyond her to my father; his face was drawn and pale. . . .

I followed the houseboy to my room, wanting to ask *him* what was wrong. I changed from my suit to a summery dress, and came out to the courtyard garden.

And there I was met with such a scene of fright and anger . . .

I listened, I heard, and I could not believe my ears. I had, on the plane, considered another woman, a divorce, as the last possible thing that could have happened. But I had not, I never would have, considered that trouble could come to my father through his profession.

That had always been like one of the sharp, gleaming knives in his instrument cases. No shadow, no spot, could ever appear on it.

But it had appeared. It was there.

For the rest of that afternoon, and again after dinner, which was served formally, as always, with the conversation held to impersonal things — Texas weather, mild gossip about friends. But after dinner, we talked again, quietly if we could, with agitation often — with panic and anger often taking over, and always threatening.

I had kept in touch with my parents. I had seen them, and written to them every two weeks. I had talked to them on the telephone. But now I knew that I had not been told the important things. For two years our communication had been on the dinner table level. Truthful, but our talks had not covered the really important things. I was on the verge of protesting this cover-up when I realized that I had been doing exactly the same thing to them.

I had never told them about Michael, about my marriage. I had "changed addresses." My telephone number was different. . . .

I gasped and tried to comprehend all the facts that now were being poured over me. I could not believe what I heard. . . .

I even found a notepad and wrote down the various items. "To get things straight," I explained to my watching parents.

I knew I wanted the facts down for me to look at and think about. I must have them to tell Michael — briefly, I was trying to figure out a way to telephone to him. I must list the things my parents wanted me to do for them.

I had been there for less than an hour when Mother said something about my staying on now with them.

I shook my head. "I can't do that," I said firmly.

But that was the only time I felt firm about anything.

I kept rejecting the truth of what was being told me. My father, I was sure, had been doing well professionally. It was nonsense to say that he had not. This was some wry joke. Or trick, even.

As for conflict in the clinic, that was easier to believe. I had, before leaving California, guessed that group practice was not for him. He was trained to think for himself, to act on his own initiative. But I had not known that he had left the clinic.

"When?" I asked.

"A year ago." He had gone into private practice, he had attained a couple of hospital affiliations — yes, he had been busy. The practice built up rather quickly, as such things went.

"And then that woman had to die!" Mother burst out. "Her family didn't know that people do die. . . ."

Father regarded her sadly, but he did not go to her, he did not say that we should speak of other things. . . .

He just sat in his chair there on the white gravel patio and looked sad. Weary.

My throat was thick. "What happened?" I asked.

Then followed minutes, stretching into an hour, of frenzied outcries against the tremendous awards being given by juries to people who thought — "Who are *led* to think, Paul!" cried Mother — that the doctor had caused the death of a patient.

I knew about the awards. Malpractice insurance was a large part of Michael's and my budget. But — had Father . . . ? Had some jury awarded . . . ?

Hadn't he carried insurance?

I took a deep breath. "What happened?" I asked again.

Father jumped up out of his chair. "I don't want to talk about it!" he cried.

But that would not do, I protested. I had come hundreds of miles to talk about what was troubling them. Mother agreed with me. "You know, dear, that we decided to ask Joey to help us."

This gave me another jolt. And a big one. Did they really expect Michael and me — My father was *rich!* He had always been rich.

"Please tell me," I begged. "The whole thing — from the beginning. Or from the time you went into private practice."

Mother sat back, nodding, her face tired and drawn. Gray. It had looked that way after Tread's death — so this must be very bad.

Father — well, his appearance was more a falling away from the meticulous grooming which he had always maintained. His hair was just a bit shaggy, he wore a white shirt open at the throat, and no jacket. One might not have noticed these things in anyone else. But with my father . . .

"Tell me," I said again.

"These things hit a fellow in private practice very hard, Joey," Father finally began to tell me.

"But you had insurance . . ."

"Oh, yes. And had I been guilty of negligence or malpractice — ignorance even —"

"You weren't, dear," breathed Mother.

"Let him talk!" I said, sounding more like Alice Peck than myself. But I had allotted two days for this visit, and —

Father was ranting again about the size of the awards.

I finally managed to get him back on the track. "Yes," he agreed, mopping his face. "Well — I had this patient. She had a violent — and of course unexpected — reaction to the injection of dyes that are commonly used for showing, with X-ray, the inside of the kidneys."

"Kidneys?" I asked. Father was still a "gut" man. Wasn't he?

Father waved his hand in dismissal of that subject.

"If I — or a member of my family —" he cried angrily, "should suffer such a reaction, I would not think of suing the doctor and the hospital. I would know that thousands of such injections are given to thousands of patients without trouble. When one patient gets a bad reaction, it is because, for some unknown reason, that patient is sensitive to the dye. She is to blame, if there is any blame to be placed."

"The lawyers said he should not have taken the risk," said Mother.

"But . . ." I protested.

Father nodded. He clapped his hands loudly together. "Precisely!" he shouted. "The chance of injuring one patient is the chance we doctors must take if we are to go ahead and save the lives of thousand of people. We doctors know that."

"Then, why . . . ?"

"Juries," said my father, speaking precisely, distinctly, his blue eyes glittering. "Juries are not made up of doctors, Joey. Juries are made up of laymen who know very little about the subject on which they must decide. And who pay no attention whatever to what the experts tell them.

"I can only decide that, in this case, the jury thought they were doing a very nice thing for the woman who was hurt, and they decided that the insurance companies which would have to pay most of the bill could absorb the blow. They don't realize that their high awards make the insurance companies raise their rates, and the doctors and hospitals must charge the patients, perhaps members of that very jury, much higher rates to be cared for when they are sick."

I nodded. This was a truth which all doctors knew and worried about.

"How much . . . ?" I asked.

"They awarded this woman and her family two hundred thousand dollars from me, and as much from the hospital crazy enough to have me on its staff."

"Oh, *Father!*"

"Yes! My insurance won't quite cover that, of course. I am in a position not to get further insurance. Hospitals will be careful not to give me further affiliation. . . ."

We spent an hour exclaiming over the disaster. But finally I asked Father what he was going to do.

There was appeal, he said. He could sell the house "back home" to pay for the cost of an appeal. Then he could go elsewhere and join a clinic or open an office. . . .

What did he want of me? My advice would be as worthless as any money I could offer.

But I knew the situation was serious. Father must find a way to continue his career. And if I could help —

I waited to be told what help he expected.

And finally I was told. He wondered . . . Did I believe . . . ? He wished, of course, that he had never dissolved his partnership with Winter.

"He would have kept me out of this in the first place," he confessed glumly.

"But — how, Father?"

"I don't know. If I knew, I would have kept myself out." He fairly snapped at me. Mother put her hand consolingly on my arm.

I smiled at her. If Father, or she, would only tell me what they wanted me to do. I had already told them that I would not stay on.

It was getting late. I was tired. Mother, at least, must be exhausted.

Finally I asked, "What is it you thought I could do?"

Father looked at me, startled. "Yes," he said, "that is what we started to tell you. To ask you . . ." He edged forward on his chair.

"You see, Joey," he said. "I have decided that I must go back home and sell the property there. And I want you to go with me. Your mother is not able. The emotional strain, the physical one, would be entirely too much for her."

So that was it. To start, anyway.

I wanted to help him, of course, though I

certainly did not see how I could. Father was not feeble. He could certainly handle the business matter of selling the house.

And I wanted to go back to Michael, to my ordered life with him. But I could not say that. Oh, I did bitterly regret that I had kept my marriage a secret. Now, all I could say was that I could not be too long away from my job. I told about the blood work I had stopped doing three months ago — and I talked quite a bit about heart surgery. Then I suggested that we were all tired. Could we leave the final plans until morning?

We went to bed. I decided to delay calling Michael until early the next morning. Then my parents would surely be asleep, and I could probably catch Michael before he left for the hospital.

I spent some sleepless time getting things together in my mind so that I could tell him quickly, and yet make him understand. When I did go to sleep, I was fearful of oversleeping.

But things worked out. I put in my call, and Michael's voice came through. "Dr. Broughton!" As I had heard him answer the phone dozens of times. Clearly, strongly.

"Oh, Michael . . ." I breathed.

"Joey? Are you all right?"

257

"I'm fine, darling. But listen . . ."

"What in cat's name do you think I'm doing?"

I laughed, then I told him. And he, too, asked what I could possibly do.

"Moral support is the only thing I can figure," I said.

"Yes, of course. It is a nasty mess, but any doctor could get into one just like it. So — you go on with him, Joey. You do what you can for him."

"He looks terrible, Michael. So — so haggard."

"I'll bet. Did you tell him . . . ?"

"Not yet, but I certainly wish he knew!"

"Yeah, yeah. It would keep you from stubbing your own toe. What did you do with your rings? Swallow them?"

I was feeling better. "Of course," I told him. "What else?"

He chuckled. "Don't lose 'em. That constitutes divorce in Texas."

So, on the second day, Father and I left for the mid-west. On the plane I managed to get him to talk a little about what he expected of me, and of Uncle Doc.

"Winter is very well thought of," said my father. "Perhaps he can put pressure to bear and get the award reduced. If enough doctors speak up on that subject . . ."

I made a note on my little white pad.

"For another thing," said Father, "I must go into practice elsewhere . . ."

"Do you mean you want to return to your partnership with Uncle Doc?"

He sighed. "No. The split between us was too great, the words spoken too bitter. But he could give me some leads, if he'd want to."

I was supposed to make him want to.

Father talked about money. And he said he really needed to get some. Lawyers' fees had already cost him a fortune. Yes, the insurance company had their men, but — And if he got an appeal, he would need money for that. Oh, yes, he had some funds, though his new practice had not yet become fully established. Now if he would need to make another change . . . What that change would be was most important.

This brought us around again to the matter of Uncle Doc. I felt he could go to his old friend himself, more effectively —

"Accept my judgment, Joey," he said, with a flash of his old self-confidence. Not quite the old arrogance, but he was sure I would be the right means of approach.

We were to stay at the hotel, and that alone brought back such a flood of memories! As did Knaup's on the corner, and of course our home.

Hermann had taken good care of it, but the place showed disuse. Mother and Father had taken many personal things with them, but there still were items . . .

The yellow chiffon dress I had worn as maid of honor for Cynthia still hung in the guest room closet. Mother's furs were in the cedar closet.

Father told me that he would cope with the real estate dealer who had a couple of prospects to buy the house. If I would see Uncle Doc as soon as possible, it would free both of us. . . .

"He'll know about my trouble," said Father. "An award of that ridiculous size gets into all the journals."

I supposed so, though Michael was often too busy to read them carefully.

"Had I better ask for an appointment through his office?" I asked. "Or go out to the Village?"

By the minute I was getting more and more reluctant to seek Uncle Doc's help. I wanted to see him. I was hungry to see him! But to go begging — to admit by my approach that Father was asking favors . . . It was not the right thing to do, nor the right way.

On the second morning I went across the

street to see Uncle Doc in his office. I felt thirteen again, going with Alice Peck and Mother to have Alice's arm cast removed. I walked to the corner and crossed. I went down that side of the street, and into the Medical Building with its gold-lettered black glass. Father's name no longer shared the panel with that of Dr. Richard Winter. Well, I had known that it would not.

Benny greeted me joyously, and I went up in the elevator, then stopped short. Now on the corridor wall there was a conventional "shingle" indicating that the offices of Dr. Richard Winter were on that floor. But where was the wooden panel? What had happened to the Purgers and Sawyers sign? I was shocked. Indeed my father no longer held a place in this office!

I opened the door and went in. There were a couple of patients waiting. There were new paintings on the wall. I spoke to the receptionist. She said that Dr. Winter was at the Kehoe Center that morning; his assistant would be in at ten —

And just about then, Miss Rasmussen, his office nurse, exploded into action. Passing through, she'd seen me at the window. She came flying out, she grabbed me.

"Joey Fivecoat!" she cried. "Where did you drop from?"

Miss Belden came out, too, and we all talked at once. We covered three years in ten minutes. Then Miss Belden told me she was sorry, my Uncle Doc was at one of the neighborhood centers that morning. He'd be so sorry! Could I come back?

She kept holding me away to look at me. I was just the same, she said. Rasmussen thought I had changed. What was I doing?

I managed to get out of them what Uncle Doc was doing, and an explanation of all the talk about neighborhood centers.

Belden stopped exclaiming over Alice Peck's family to tell me that Uncle Doc had expanded his service. He never had thought doctors should wait for sick people to come to them. I'd remember? "He's lately taken over the orthopedic service of the various health centers throughout the poverty areas of the city. Examinations, surgery, therapy . . . Of course he is doing good! You know him! When he sees you, Joey, he'll put you to work!"

"Oh, I live in Texas," I said. "I have my own health service with the cardiacs."

She beamed at me. "He'll want to hear about that," she assured me. "Will you come back? Though you'd do better to go see him at home. What with the rehab and all, this place gets woolly whenever he's in the office."

I knew what she meant.

I told her that I would go out to the Village that evening.

But during the afternoon, sorting through books and personal things in our old home, I realized that I was dreading the meeting. So much, so very much, had happened! The last time I had seen Uncle Doc he had been very angry at all the Fivecoats.

But I had to see him. I had promised Father that I would. And I must do it quickly, so that things could be resolved one way or the other, and I could go home to Michael.

About three o'clock I thought of calling Alan!

He had, so far as I personally knew, not been angry with us. If he were in the phone book —

He was. His name had three listings. Alan Winter, Atty. at Law.

Oh, my!

He had a home, or maybe an apartment, in the city. And his Village phone was listed, too. His office . . . Well! I surely could find him someplace.

I tried the office first, and was put right through to him.

He was delighted to hear from me. "Joey!"

he shouted through the telephone. "Oh, my goodness, my goodness!"

Tears were pouring down my cheeks. Dear Alan . . .

"Where — when — can I see you?" he asked.

"From right now on," I told him. "And almost anywhere." I said that I was staying at the hotel. . . .

"My office is downtown. There's a bar, very respectable — Could you meet me there in an hour?"

I said, yes, of course, and hung up. I changed to a silk suit, brushed my hair and left before Father returned. I left a memo saying where I had gone . . . "To meet Alan."

The bar was indeed a respectable one. Small tables, discreet lighting — Alan was waiting for me. He hugged me bearishly. He held me away, his finger touching my hair, my cheek, the red scarf at my throat.

He was older, bigger — more solid. But his hair was just as red. "I like red-headed men," I said, gulping.

He laughed and ordered drinks.

"Now, talk!" he demanded.

We both talked. He was fine, he said. Not married. "Couldn't find any reason not to wait for you," he said with his so-well-re-membered grin.

Uncle Doc was well. Too busy, of course. His mother was not quite so well; she had sold the Village house and was living in the tenant cottage on Uncle Doc's place.

Cynthia was working as assistant curator at an art gallery in Florida.

"What does she know about art?" I asked, sounding like my old belligerent self where Cynthia was concerned.

"Not much, I suspect," said her brother loyally. "But she decorates the place. If she had some money, she'd be a prominent figure in the jet set."

I got the picture. We had her sort in Texas, too.

"Everyone has to do his thing, Joey," he reminded me.

"I know," I said. "I know. Me, too."

He pushed the bowl of cashews toward me. "Now it's your turn, Joey." His eyes searched my face.

"I live in — near — Houston," I said. "I trained as a lab technician so that I could work in a heart clinic. Alice . . ." I swept on quickly. I would not tell even a white lie to Alan. "Alice Peck is married and lives in Colorado." I told about Per and the horse ranch, and the two towheaded children — "with another planned for, I'm sure."

We reminisced about Alice and horses, we

reminisced about everything, and had a lovely time. It was truly a return to the happy days of our childhood. I had always been so fond of Alan!

But by the time I reached the bottom of my Collins glass, having sipped very slowly, I must state my reason for being in the city. We were selling the house, I said. He seemed to know about Father's "bad luck." But he shook his head when I said . . .

"Uncle Doc won't want to see Dr. Five-coat," he broke in to say gravely.

"I wish he would . . ."

Alan shrugged.

"Will he see me?"

"I don't know, Joey. But I'll ask him."

"He'll do it," I said confidently.

He smiled at me. "We all love you, Joey."

He took me to dinner, and we danced, remembering how I had always loved to dance. His arms were strong, and his shoulder warm, his cheek against my hair — When he took me to the hotel, he kissed me, and I clung to him. "I've missed you, Alan," I told him.

So he kissed me again, more strongly, more possessively.

And I went to bed, swept with the idea that I was in love with Alan. Perhaps I had always been in love with him . . . I propped myself high on pillows and thought about him, forgetting to call Michael, though I thought about him, and about my marriage. From there, with Alan's kiss still on my lips, that marriage seemed like a dream.

I drifted off into sleep, and woke to ask myself if I had made a mistake. Alan and I had so much in common. I could stay right here in the city, resume my medical studies . . . even marry . . . live at the Village . . .

I sat straight up in bed. Down below my window, the street was all but deserted. And I was insane! Completely mad! What was my plan? To divorce Michael? That was nonsense. Utter and complete.

I lay back, remembering my dream of Alan, which certainly had been physical . . .

I would call Michael at five-thirty. Alan had promised to get word to me early that morning as to whether Uncle Doc would see me.

I did call Michael, but he did not answer at home. I then called the hospital and was told that he was in surgery. I left a message, and thought again about my swift, passionate dream of Alan . . .

He telephoned me before nine. Uncle Doc, he said, had consented to see me.

"Without any commitment, Joey . . ."

"I understand that. But I do want to see him. For my own sake as much as . . ."

Alan said he would pick me up at noon, we'd have lunch. . . .

"Chicken salad sandwich and a hot fudge sundae at Knaup's?" I asked.

He laughed. "If that's what you want."

It's what we had, enjoying every delicious morsel of the food, enjoying each other.

"Am I to see Uncle Doc at his office?" I asked, realizing that Alan was giving me a lot of his time.

"No. I am to take you out to the Village."

"Oh, *Alan!*"

"Don't want to ride with me?"

I laughed. "Don't want to use your whole day," I assured him.

"When our Uncle Doc says bring — no, he said *fetch* — 'Fetch her out here at two' — he meant I was to fetch you out there at two."

So we drove out to the Village; on the way Alan told me of changes there. Several of the original families had died off — others had sold their homes, or younger members of the families had taken over. It just was not the same. For instance, the town meeting was no longer the occasion for a dinner party.

Uncle Doc kept only one horse, "for senti-mental reasons."

"Alice's horse?"

Yes, it was.

"I'll tell her. She'll probably come to see it."

"He'd love that. He loved you girls."

But not Tread. Well . . .

For the last ten minutes, I sat silent. I was feeling strange. I could not be sure if I was frightened or just terribly excited. My pulse rate had quickened. The mirror showed that my color had paled. I felt a thickness in my throat and butterflies trembled in my stom-ach; there was a dryness in my mouth.

I touched Alan's arm. "I'm scared," I told him. Every bodily function was telling me to fight, or run. Everything had slowed down to give preference, I supposed, to the most urgently needed muscles.

Alan smiled at me and pulled up at the terrace door of Uncle Doc's home. Sunlight washed it, sparkled from the windows, added brilliance to the flowers . . .

"He'll be right inside," he told me.

"Aren't you . . . ?"

"Got to get back on the job. Love, Joey!"

And he drove away, leaving me in my blue skirt, and striped blouse, my white shoes, to go up the steps, open the terrace door and go into Uncle Doc's sunroom. There was a large painting of yellow iris on the brick wall above the comfortable, big leather couch. There was a bowl of blue and pink cosmos daisies and Queen Anne's lace on the glass-topped table, and Uncle Doc was coming out of the house toward me, his arms out-stretched.

"Little Joey," he said warmly. "Dear little Joey!"

He hugged me, then held me away as Alan had done. "I like the short hair," he said. "Better than the horns . . . Remember?"

"Weren't they terrible?" I asked.

"Yes, they were. Here, let's sit down. We'll have a good talk."

He had not changed. His fringe of hair had long been white. The bulk of his body may have sagged somewhat. But his skin was firm, and his blue eyes were as keen as ever.

He was very kind and warm to me, and said that I had always been the "best of the lot."

"Oh, no, I'm not," I said, no longer afraid or even excited. It was just the old Village happiness that held me in a bubble of clear glass.

I told him about Alice Peek, about the babies. . . .

"Both boys, Uncle Doc, with fat, sturdy

legs, and heads of curly yellow hair. You can't tell them from the puppies on the ranch house porch. She plans to have a third baby next year, which she says had better be a girl!"

"So she can ride the horses!" agreed Uncle Doc, laughing. "Good for Alice! Now, how about you? Have you got your degree?"

I looked at him in surprise. "Oh, no," I said.

"Why not?"

"Well, for one thing, a lot has happened."

He grunted.

But he would not let me talk about my father.

"What are *you* doing?" he asked me.

"Well," I began, "I stayed with the folks in California for a year, then I went to Texas and got a lab job in one of the heart clinics. . . ."

He leaned toward me, his eyes probing my face. "You went to Texas on your own?" he asked. "To a strange, big city . . ."

"I loved the work, Uncle Doc."

He sat back. "Well, good for you, Joey," he cried. "Good for you!"

"That's why," I attempted, "I didn't know that Father . . ."

He held up his big, clean, surgeon's hand.

"Things take strange turns, Joey," he said sadly. "It is hard to say what small thing, or even what big thing, makes the difference.

"Back in history, there was Richelieu. The father of what is called the French civilization. Was he the cause of that, or the obscure surgeon who, when he was at the point of death, gave him ten years of life to do the things he did? Who is responsible for modern air conditioning? The pioneer inventor or the assassin of President Garfield?"

I settled down happily into the corner of the couch. This was the Uncle Doc I remembered.

"Who gave Britain the victory at Trafalgar?" he went on. "Nelson or the young naval surgeon who amputated his arm and let him live to win that battle? Would we have had World War One if a faulty diagnosis had not hastened the death of the emperor that put old Kaiser Bill on the throne?

"Little things change our lives, Joey. Relatively little things. They cause the domino action which makes history. In the nation, and in our personal lives."

I stirred.

"Take Garfield's assassination," he swept on. "The President survived the bullet for eighty hot, humid, typically Washington summer days. Something had to be done, and an obscure scientist-inventor came up with the device needed. He installed a fan to blow over a cake of ice. It cooled the air without removing the moisture. And sepsis caused the President's death. So! It became an open question as to whether the assassin's bullet killed Garfield or the well-meaning physicians who repeatedly probed the wound with their fingers to determine the course of the bullet."

He paused. Then he said thoughtfully, "They would have been judged guilty of malpractice today."

I sighed. "Father needs your help, Uncle Doc," I told him.

"Yes. I understand that he does. Help of some kind, at any rate. Of course, what happened to him could happen to any doctor." Michael had said that. "But the award was impossible!"

"He feels — we all feel — that if he had stayed here with you, if he could have stayed, he would never have got into trouble."

Uncle Doc mopped his flushed face with a big white handkerchief. "He's right about that!" he cried. "The man isn't a urologist! What in Tom Thunder was he doing with the kidneys?"

I didn't know. I said that, maybe, at the trial it had hurt him if anyone testified that

273

he was not a kidney specialist. I looked up at Uncle Doc.

"I went to your office," I said. "What has happened to the Purgers and Sawyers sign?"

He looked surprised. "Your father took it with him when he removed his personal possessions, Joey."

"I hope he still has it. I want it."

"When you ask him for it, tell him to stay with what he knows, Joey. And that's the gut."

"He hoped you would help him . . ."

"It's high time he learned to take care of himself."

"He thinks the award might be reduced."

"The AMA would be the ones to get to work on that. What does he plan to do now? Stay in California?"

"He's sold our house here. And — No, he wants to move somewhere. You wouldn't know of something? Please?"

He smiled at me. "No, dear. It is entirely up to him. He should pull up his own socks. He's a very good doctor. The best, in fact. He knows that, and he can get himself out of this when he's settled down to the acknowledgment of that fact."

I nodded. "I'll have to tell him," I said. "Of course you'd know all about what happened to him?"

"Sure, I know. There's been a lot written and said. We condemn these juries. But most of us keep out of such big messes. Your father may now have learned to know that, and act upon it. He'll find something. Maybe not the posh practice he's accustomed to having, but there is work for him to do. Tell him — not from me, but from you — to look into this emergency room work. It's a new and big thing, Joey. We specialist fellows forget that the family doctor has been about phased out, and that, in the cities, the emergency room has had to take its place. This situation will get worse. Already, big hospitals are putting some fine men in there to make the primary diagnoses. Paul might look into that.

"Now! Let's talk about you."

I sat smiling at him. "Things are wonderful with me," I told him. And for the first time, except with Alice, I could talk to my "family" about Michael and my marriage. As I talked, I realized how good a marriage it was. I told about Michael's work . . .

"He'll be one of the big heart men, I'm sure," I said. "Even now he heads a team. He works in surgery all day several days a week. He had many ideas for the heart-lung setup, he thinks there will be great advances in pacesetters and artificial valves. Even artificial hearts sometime . . ."

Uncle Doc sat and watched me. He did not approve of my keeping still about my marriage.

"I was afraid something would spoil it for me," I said quietly.

He nodded in understanding. "You say you work in a clinic lab?"

"I did. And I loved it. Michael says I should go on and get my M.D."

"Why don't you?"

I laughed, and I am sure I blushed. "I think he'd rather I'd go into applied obstetrics."

"How about you?" Uncle Doc was chuckling.

"I think I'd like that, too."

"Then do it, child. Do it! And along that line, I'll give you one word of advice."

I waited, watching his face.

"Don't train your kids to call your Michael 'Father.' In this day and age . . . Respect is fine, respect is needed. But give them room to breathe!"

"I'll remember," I said.

"And tell me when the first one is born, will you?"

"Of course."

He sat thoughtful, still gazing at me. "You've taken a load off my mind, honey," he said then. "A big load. You see — last night — Alan came out here pretty late and told me that you were in town and wanted to see me."

"Yes. I first went to your office . . ."

"Mhmmmn. And I don't know that I'd have seen you at all. For the purpose you had. But with Alan — I was afraid maybe we were going to have a problem with you two."

"I've always been fond of him, Uncle Doc."

"I knew that. We all knew that. And the way he talked last night — babbled, was the way it was — I got the idea . . ."

I blushed again, remembering my dream. "You wouldn't want anything like that to develop, would you?" I asked. "Not even if I were free."

"We couldn't handle it, Joey. Not any of us. Not even you and Alan. There are too many things to forgive and forget."

He was right, of course. He had always been one to see the whole picture.

"No," he repeated. "It would not do. You put all your love into the marriage you have, give it to the man you chose. Make your life with him. Your own life, dear. I can see half a dozen paths ahead for you. The babies, or you could go on and get your M.D. Or help your Michael with his work. You'd be a great help. Maybe you could do all three. But, mainly, I hope you have his children."

I nodded, and got to my feet. I touched a vase, I lifted a familiar paperweight to my cheek. "I should be leaving," I said, "but I have always hated to leave your house."

"You are welcome here at any time. Bring Michael and the kids."

I smiled at him. "They'd love it," I said. "They'd love you. Even if you won't help their grandfather."

"No," said Uncle Doc. "And I don't think I should even try, Joey. Oh, well, maybe a little. In the background."

I understood. Richard Winter's word here, his word there, could help any man.

He saw that I understood. "But I'll do that, Joey, only if he helps himself. It has bothered me that I have never been able to forgive him because he let my girl marry Tread. I cannot believe that he did not know what that boy was."

"Maybe not," I said. "Maybe he truly did not know. Father has always lived in an A Apple Pie world, a world without dimension or reality."

Uncle Doc looked at me oddly. "How long have you known that?" he asked.

"The knowledge came slowly. I recognized

it first when I was worrying about Cynthia and Tread. She wanted to get married, and she did everything she could — I found I couldn't talk to my father about what was happening."

"Did *you* know that Tread . . . ?"

"No, only that he didn't want to be married the way Cynthia did. He was a sweet boy, and always tried to please people."

"Hmmmm," said Uncle Doc. "I wish you had told me at the time."

"I should have."

"It changes things a little. Enough that — if Paul does help himself out of this mess, maybe — But then, in that case, he won't need my help, will he? And that's the best way, Joey. Isn't it?"

I left then, without seeing Alan again. The yardman was to drive me back to the city. I clung to Uncle Doc when I told him good-by. "I'm so glad," I said, "that you haven't changed! You know? My main and only plan is to have Christmases in our home like the ones you gave us here."

This pleased him. He closed the car door.

"Thank you for explaining," I said softly, as we drove away. "Thank you. . . ."

At the hotel, I gave Father the two messages of advice which Uncle Doc had had for him. He agreed to put his appeal into the hands of the Medical Association. They were definitely opposed to making such huge awards a precedent. But as for emergency room service . . .

"I am still a gastric specialist," he said stiffly.

I went into my room and began to pack my bag. "I must leave in the morning," I said over my shoulder. "I am needed at home." And I told him of my marriage, of Michael. He accepted that quietly, too.

But when he took me to the plane, he said, "Bring Michael to see us, Joey. . . ."

"You come and see how this looks beside our front door," I answered, shifting the Purgers and Sawyers sign in my arms. Father had found it for me; he had put it away in a cupboard in the library.

Michael, his red hair glinting in the sun, met my plane, and I was very glad to see him, to be lifted in his strong arms. Of course it was Michael I loved! My brief dream of Alan, that was nostalgia. Michael held me long and close. I looked up into his face, and I saw the relief in his eyes. Had he feared I would not return?

But of course I would. Of course I had.

I'd been crazy even to have been disturbed by Alan. He was dear to me, he always would be dear. Like a brother . . .

Michael got my bag, and we walked out to the car. "You told your father, I hope," he said sternly, "about me."

"I had to," I said. "If we start having a family, he'd have to know."

He smiled then.

"Don't drive so fast, Michael," I breathed.

"Why not? I have to get back on the job to take care of — A *family?* Wow!"

Chapter 12

It was fifteen years before I fully realized my dreams for Christmas. It was fifteen years before Mother and Father, Alice and her family, all could be with us for the holiday.

But from the first one, I began to work on Christmases in our home. I tried to make them all that the Village had given me in the way of joy and happiness and fulfillment. We had the big tree, the big feast, the special gifts, the perfume, the noise, the peaceful happiness of Christmas.

And when our oldest son was fourteen, we finally got the whole family together. Things had changed for all of us. Alice was a bit more than pleasantly plump, and no one of her four children minded. Nor did Per, still big, blond, and silent. He enjoyed the burro which was the pet of our family.

Our big, clean, functional home expanded well to contain so many guests. Mother and Father, of course, were made comfortable in the master bedroom. All the children — seven of them — slept in dormitory rooms — four boys in one, the three little girls in the other. Though *slept* perhaps was not the word to use.

The guests from Colorado, Mother and Father from the east, enjoyed the warm sunshine, the flower beds and the wide lawns outside our wide windows, as I knew, and planned, that they would.

Alice teased me about not having a palm Christmas tree. "Remember how we objected to one in the Bahamas?"

Michael worried lest I do too much in the way of preparation. "If I could help . . ." he fretted.

He could not help. Michael had been named Chief of the Children's Cardiovascular Unit of the big center. He had directional duties as well as the surgery which he performed, and loved to perform. He was the sort of doctor to take each patient into his heart and mind. Of *course* he was too busy to hang wreaths and heap oranges into a wooden bowl, to plan and shop for stocking gifts.

But I had help. The cook in the kitchen brought in her granddaughter to set tables and clear them. To make beds. Our by-the-day boy would come every day to keep the stone patio swept, the pool clean, flowers cut for the house.

I made lists and lists, and wrote notes

reminding me of things to be done.

"You are working too hard," said Michael over and over again.

"I'm happy."

"That makes it worthwhile?"

"Of course. I only wish Uncle Doc could be here."

"He'll come another time. He's a great guy."

He was. He had been in our home, and he would come again.

Two days before Christmas, I met Father and Mother's plane. I remembered to wear a plaid wool skirt, a white blouse and sweater. I had had my short hair trimmed. I laughed with joy and some dismay at my first sight of my parents. They too had changed. Mother's beautifully dressed hair was silver gray. Father's only glinted with gold. Both wore handsomely tailored suits, they carried topcoats, and had felt hats on their heads. Not many people in Texas wore hats socially.

They admired our home. Father nodded at the Purgers and Sawyers sign over the fireplace, and asked when Alice Peck would arrive.

"Tonight or tomorrow morning. They are driving."

"All that distance?" asked Mother.

"Colorado isn't too far from Texas, Mother. Besides, we think in terms of hundred miles."

When the Andersson station wagon rolled in the next day, my children's nicely constrained good manners blew to the winds. Four cousins to show things to — seven children to race through the house — to ride the burro, to fly a model airplane, to go walking down to the main road for the mail . . .

Seven children, and their parents, their grandparents to go to church on Christmas Eve, with our little girl falling asleep within the circling arm of her beloved daddy, and needing to be carried out like a sack of wheat.

Seven children to awaken at dawn, wanting to explore their stockings and open the gifts piled beneath the shining tree. Seven to be asked to wait until Grandfather and Grandmother were up and dressed, ready to watch them do it.

Michael and Alice were almost as anxious, and I served everyone hot chocolate and oranges to hold them until the bedroom door should open.

As it did open, of course, and Mother and Father came out, neatly dressed for the day, surprised at the shout of welcome which greeted them.

Of course, then the day swept along of its own momentum. The familiar noise and welter of paper and string, with a puppy getting into the house by mistake adding to the excitement. Children's voices rang like bells, there was a tear or two, a sober minute or so . . .

"It's good," said Per to me as we watched.

I smiled up at him. "I thought it would be."

Food was served. A huge breakfast, with nobody being too strict about the children's staying at table. And then the preparations for the big dinner at four. A turkey roasting, a ham baking, ruby cranberry sauce sparkling in a bowl on a side table — the house smelled like Uncle Doc's, Alice assured me. "How did you keep the tacos out? I can't, at home."

"It took doing," I agreed.

"Your Michael loves it, doesn't he?"

"I'd not have him around if he wouldn't."

The ten-speed bikes were tried out. The little girls played with their new dolls, though Alice's older daughter said she liked her shoe skates better.

"She's exactly like you," I told my sister.

"Goodness! I'll have to do something about that!"

Per took the children for the ritual walk before dinner. Mother and Father took a nap while Alice and I saw to the last items for the feast. Michael went in to the hospital, promising faithfully to be back.

He was. Everyone was ready for dinner, the little girls in pretty frocks, the boys in clean shirts and shining faces. "The Broughtons do run to freckles," Alice teased me.

"I don't see any brunettes among the Anderssons," I retorted.

Michael presided at his own table, big, sure of himself as a successful doctor and family man. He said grace, and carved the turkey. Mother and Father sat halfway down one side of the long table, Alice and Per across from them. My two boys and my curly-headed four-year-old — Paul, Dick, and Christine — were delighted at the fun in their home. Red heads, freckles — I was proud of them. As Alice was of her brood who were just enough older — blond, handsome, and strong. Paul again, and Peter. The lovely, blonde little girls. Joey and Margretta.

"It's a grand family," I said contentedly.

Alice's Paul took pictures. I would send one to Uncle Doc.

After dessert was served and Michael carried the plum pudding ablaze around the table, Father announced that he had something to say.

"A speech!" groaned Peter Andersson.

"This one will be worth hearing," his father assured the boy.

Father bowed slightly. "And it will be short," he promised his grandson. "I wish only to announce to my family that I have decided to retire."

Our heads snapped up. He had not said a word of this to any of us.

"A surgeon who does the delicate work I do loses his dexterity after a certain age. I would not work in less than a dexterous fashion."

He had been doing exceedingly well with his "dexterous" surgery. Indeed, he had become exceedingly well known for the shunt-by-pass intestinal operation he had helped develop and perfect for obese patients.

Now he spoke whimsically of that success, of his repute. He laughed at this turn in his career. "I did not invent the technique," he said. "I never have approved of it — and I still do not. But I have tried to go along with the tide of years. As you know, I have survived that ultimate crisis which marks success for a busy surgeon. I have been sued for malpractice and won the suit."

He had. He had won it for himself. A patient had died after willingly, voluntarily undergoing surgery to lose weight. That surgery involved removal of a part of the small intestine to allow food to pass through the body more quickly, and to limit its absorption. This weight was lost regardless of how much food was consumed.

"I have done, I do, better and more significant surgery," Father was saying. "Now it is time for me to say I shall do no more of any kind. I shall do some consulting and writing. Your mother and I shall travel . . ."

Mother sat there beside him, the look on her face Alice and I knew so well. Still loving, still adoring.

I mentioned this to Michael when I began to fill coffee cups.

"That's the way she should be," he told me.

I opened my lips, ready to dispute him. He put his strong fingers on my wrist. "For her, Joey. Not you."

"I adore you," I whispered, happy again.

"When I deserve it," he agreed smugly.

Ice cream was brought in for the smaller children who preferred it to the pudding. And Father, benignly, asked Alice's boys, then mine, what they planned to do with their lives.

My Paul said he would study medicine, and remembered to add "Sir." Dick said he wanted to play football.

"That makes three quarterbacks in the family," laughed Alice.

Father was very pleased, however, to have Paul announce for medicine. In his old manner of taking over and deciding things, he said, "Come home with me, son! I'll see that you get the proper education. Both of you boys may come, if you like. We'll devote our full time to it. I've always felt guilty that I did not encourage your mother when she wanted to study medicine, that I didn't help her and make her stay with it." He beamed at me.

"Now I can rid myself of any guilt. I have no son left, but if you'd allow me to take Paul, I would guide his training. In the old, strict way, Michael. Not giving way to the frills and short cuts that the medical schools want us to believe in now."

I could see, all too vividly, the picture of our old life for my son, a life carefully planned, and always proper. There would be the trips, the museums, and music. His friends would be selected, his clothes . . .

Michael and I listened, Alice Peck did, her blue eyes very round, her face bright and watchful.

I saw the pity in my good husband's eyes. He squeezed my hand. "Now, Joey," he murmured.

I nodded. "No, Father," I said firmly. "This is our family. We'll keep it together, the way a family should be. You'll agree?"

"Yes," said Father. "Ye-es."

"We love you. That is why Alice and I each named our sons for you. But they still must be our sons."

"Yes," said Father. But he was hurt, and I was sorry. "It's so easy to make mistakes, Joey," he said anxiously.

"Yes, it is. But, please, dear, we'll make our own. And live with them."

"You don't know what you are talking about!" he cried, almost angrily.

"Yes, we do," I said. "Oh, yes, indeed we do!"

We hope you have enjoyed this Large Print book. Other Thorndike Press or Chivers Press Large Print books are available at your library or directly from the publishers.

For more information about current and upcoming titles, please call or write, without obligation, to:

Thorndike Press
P.O. Box 159
Thorndike, Maine 04986 USA
Tel. (800) 257-5157

OR

Chivers Press Limited
Windsor Bridge Road
Bath BA2 3AX
England
Tel. (0225) 335336

All our Large Print titles are designed for easy reading, and all our books are made to last.